The Second Man

MERLINE LOVELACE

Alena

Harlequin Books

TORONTO • NEW YORK • LONDON
AMSTERDAM • PARIS • SYDNEY • HAMBURG
STOCKHOLM • ATHENS • TOKYO • MILAN
MADRID • WARSAW • BUDAPEST • AUCKLAND

ISBN 0-373-28820-4

ALENA

Copyright © 1994 by Merline Lovelace.

This edition published by arrangement with Harlequin Enterprises B. V.

® and TM are trademarks of the publisher. Trademarks indicated with
® are registered in the United States Patent and Trademark Office, the
Canadian Trade Marks Office and in other countries.

Printed in U.S.A.

Also by Steve Martini

The Second Man

A PAUL MADRIANI NOVELLA

STEVE MARTINI

WITNESS
IMPULSE

An Imprint of HarperCollins Publishers

Excerpt from *The Enemy Inside* copyright © 2015 by Steve Martini.

EPub Edition APRIL 2015 ISBN: 9780062414724
Print Edition ISBN: 9780062414731

10 9 8 7 6 5 4

Chapter 1

As I EYE him from across my desk, Cameron Akers is not what you might expect. He is not a big man. Maybe five foot ten. I would guess he weighs about 180 pounds. In his early thirties, his face is chiseled, pockmarked in a few places by what I suspect are old wounds. His arms are well toned and covered with colorful tattoos, a dragon that ripples under the muscles of one forearm and demons of someone's imagination that dance on the other.

Passing him on the street, you might not look twice, Mr. Cellophane—look right through him. Except that while you weren't looking, Cameron Akers could probably put four holes between the top of your eyes and your hairline, none of them more than half an inch apart.

According to our investigator Herman Diggs, who brought Akers into my office, Cam, as he calls him, is a career Navy SEAL. He is assigned to the BUD/S training depot a mile or so down the Silver Strand from our office here in Coronado. I am Paul Madriani, of the law firm of Madriani & Hinds. My partner Harry Hinds and I have a criminal defense practice confined mostly to cases in the state courts of California. Of late, these activities have become far more dangerous, due in part, it seems, to our proximity to the southern border with Mexico, the resulting narcotraffic, and its combination with international terrorism and the drug cartels.

"I assume Herman told you that we generally don't do cases involving military law?" I tell him.

"Told him," says Herman. "According to Cam, any charges they bring would be filed in the federal courts."

"I'm no longer in the Navy," says Akers. "Been separated about two months. Cashiered, you might call it, though the decision to leave was mine."

"What exactly are these charges?"

"Nothing yet," says Akers. "It's a long story."

"Can you give me the short version?" I ask him. "I have an appointment shortly."

"Like Herman says, my last assignment was as a BUD/S training NCO, basic underwater demolition. Navy SEAL warfare base here in Coronado. My grade was chief petty officer. The assignment was a holding pattern 'til the brass could force me out. I'm shy of twenty years, so there's no retirement, no medical coverage."

"Why did they want to force you out?"

"Before coming to Coronado, I was assigned to DEVGRU, the Naval Special Warfare Development Group . . ."

"SEAL Team Six," says Herman. "As in Abbottabad—

Pakistan." Herman, all 250 pounds of him, sits bolt upright in the other client chair across from my desk, beaming at me as if he were Akers's talent agent.

"You were there?" I look at Akers. "The mission to get bin Laden?"

He nods.

"Where did you meet Herman?" I ask.

"Oh, we met at the health club," says Herman.

"Let him talk for himself," I tell Herman.

"Chuze Fitness, down in National City," says Akers. "We got to talkin'. Herman said he worked for a law firm. I needed a lawyer."

"Go on."

"I assume by now you know the story," he says. "Operation Neptune Spear."

You would have to live on Mars not to have heard about it. "Refresh my memory."

"Everything went down pretty much the way it appeared in the newspapers," says Akers. "All forty or so various versions. It was dark, we were on the run, lots of chaos and confusion, walled-off doors and dead-end corridors. Your typical trip to armed Islam. One smashed-up bird going in, high-end Black Hawk with buffered rotors. At first it was pretty quiet. The sound of tactical boots on gravel, a few barking dogs. Then all hell broke loose. The first detonation from breaching charges to get through one of the walls. Then cinders of flashing-hot steel from somebody's grenades. Theirs or ours, I don't know. Some unsuppressed automatic fire from people inside the compound. You stop thinking and go into auto mode, all the stuff you learned in training and absorbed on missions. The stuff that keeps you alive. In the end, all the right people got shot. We all came home alive in one piece, strange as it seems. The problems came later. After the mission."

"What problems?"

"Loose lips," says Akers "Lot of people talking. It started with the politicians. They wanted to wallow in the afterglow. Some of them ID'ed Navy SEALs as the strike team, and from there it all went downhill. The media pounced on Team Six, started hanging in bars where sources told them some of the squad bent elbows from time to time. Strangers would show up and buy rounds of drinks. Media was everywhere, knocking on every door, looking for information.

"And it got worse. A feature film was green-lighted by the White House. Hollywood producers demanded access to details. The president's people wanted to fire up the limelight for the reelection campaign. The film director demanded specifics on means and methods. Wanted to know how we did it, all the little details, stuff he could put in the movie for color. Except once he did that, how could we use the same techniques the next time? Didn't matter. Not to the powers in Washington. Our people were told to deliver. It's all buried now. All the compromising dirty little e-mails, deep in the bowels at the CIA."

"Why there?" I ask.

"Neptune Spear was a CIA operation," says Akers.

"I didn't know that."

"Most people don't. The CIA is a cosmic sucking black hole. Information that goes there never comes out. The agency is totally exempt from Freedom of Information demands. If you're the president, you want all your darkest secrets and biggest mistakes filed there. Let me put it this way. If Cain had murdered Abel at Langley, God would still be asking who did it."

"I get the picture."

"Do you? To make a long story short, it became impossible to maintain operational security. The brass was furious. Some of the operators started to worry about their families, others caught the disease and started talking. One of them wrote a book, another came out of the shadows and declared that he was the man who shot bin Laden."

"Did he?"

"Did he what?"

"Shoot the man."

Akers shrugs a shoulder, looks at me, and says: "Who knows? You won't hear it from me. I don't talk."

"You just have."

"Only about things that are already revealed. In the public wheelhouse, as they say."

"According to the stories I've read, it was the second man up the stairs into bin Laden's bedroom who shot him," I say.

"Maybe. But who was the second man? And does it really matter? Think of it as a fiesta," says Akers. "Blindfolded, looking through the tunnel that is night vision, packing heat, squeezing off occasional rounds at anything that looked hostile and moved. When you take off the blindfold, there's candy all over the floor. Do you really care who broke the piñata?"

"Perhaps history does."

"Any one of us could have put a bullet in the man's turban. Rumor has it, and I'm not confirming this, that by the time they got the body back to Bagram, it had more holes in it than your average colander. Nobody is ever going to know all the details of what happened that night. All you're gonna get is one man's story of what he thinks he saw."

"The fog of war?" I say.

"Nature of the mission," says Akers. "We were after the devil. If it even looks like it wiggles, shoot it."

"Did you?"

"Can't remember," he says. "Let's not talk about operational details. That's why I'm in trouble," he says. "It's why they forced me out. They think I've talked, and I haven't."

"Who's 'they'?"

"The brass."

"Have you talked to anybody about the details of this particular mission, or anything else for that matter?"

"NO!

"Family, friends, other members of the team?"

"No one!" he says.

"Did anybody talk to you about it?"

"A few operators. People who were pissed off about the leaks, same as I am."

"So you did commiserate?"

"Shop talk," he says. "All of it in-house. On the base with people who were there on the mission. Nothing outside. Most of the others have been washed out, too. Sent off to other assignments. Detached from DEVGRU."

"So you're not alone in this?"

"No."

"Why would they do this? The brass, I mean?"

"Who knows? Political fallout. A lot of paranoia. Higher-ups were furious about the leaks, particularly operational details on tactics and methods. Once disclosed, they couldn't be used again. The politicians, especially the ones who fingered us after the mission and were called on it were busy looking to blame someone else. There is talk that the Justice Department is working up a case against some members of the squadron. Violation of the agreement signed by us."

"What agreement?"

"Nondisclosure," says Akers. "Violation carries criminal penalties. In the end, we come away with nothing. No pension, no medical coverage for ourselves or our families, and no security or protection in the event of retaliation by the enemy. We're left bare, all of us in the same situation, with the threat of criminal prosecution now hanging over our heads. It's not just me. It's my family," he says.

"It's not fair" says Herman.

"Tell me about your family?" I say.

"My wife and two boys, six and eight. If I go to prison, what's gonna happen to them? If I'm prosecuted in open court, identified as being part of the mission, and some fanatic of a lone wolf decides to take revenge, who protects my wife and kids while I'm in jail?"

It's a good question. One for which I have no answer.

"Knowing all this, why did you get out of the military? Why not tough it out and retire? At least take the benefits?"

"I didn't leave by choice. You don't understand. Let me explain. Among the SEAL teams, DEVGRU, what you know as SEAL Team Six, is the peak of the pyramid. It took me six years to get there, a tough, hard climb. Once you get there, you're called on to participate in countless missions over long years, all of them dangerous. You don't ask questions, you do it because it's what you do. Then to have all of that taken away, to be reassigned to BUD/S training because of scuttlebutt that somebody is talking and your name got mentioned and now your career is over, that's what happened. No matter what I do, what I say, I know it's over. There is no coming back from this. On paper, it may look like I quit. The fact is I had no other alternative. You know the military, the Navy, they can get rid of anybody they want anytime they want. They let it be known that if I stayed, they would bring charges. Probably a court-martial. They would see to it I got a dishonorable discharge. I'd lose everything anyway."

"They told you this?"

"Not in so many words. But the message was clear."

"So what is it you want us to do?"

"I want my life back," he says.

"You want to be reinstated in the military?"

"That's never going happen," says Akers. "But I'd like to be able to move on. Make the criminal thing go away and find a decent job."

This would seem a reasonable request. Still, I don't know all the facts or what motivates the people in power.

"Are you working now?"

"I was, until two weeks ago. The FBI came snooping, asking questions of my employer. I was on probation. They cut me loose."

"What type of work?"

"Sheriff's department up in Orange County. As you can imagine, there is a limited demand for the skill set you develop jumping out of helicopters and shooting people for a decade and a half. Police agencies might take a look. But not when the FBI keeps stopping in to ask questions.

"There is Blackwater and some of its subsidiaries, private security companies hired by government agencies overseas. The problem is, you have a bigger target on your chest with fewer assets at your back. The pay is all right, but the mortality table is awful. Besides, as you get older, you get burned-out. You can only do this stuff so long and stay alive."

"I understand. Why didn't you think about this before you enlisted?"

"I was nineteen years old. I was young and stupid, like everybody else. The equivalent of being immortal," says Akers. "If you make it through the training phase, which is about 1 percent, you figure you'll probably be lucky to survive the first few missions. By the time you're older, it's too late. By then, you're in for the duration—death, disability, or retirement. Or what happened to me."

"It's enough to make anyone angry," says Herman. "The government is getting ready to shower billions in benefits on millions of people who entered the country illegally. The same time, it's turning its back on men who risked their lives every day on the battlefield."

This is all very true. Still, I can hear my law partner Harry Hinds, the two inevitable questions he will ask: "What can we possibly do for this man? And more to the point, how is he going to pay us?"

Akers answers the first as if by telepathy before I can speak. "If you can get the government off my back, make the threat of prosecution and the FBI go away, I can take care of the rest," he says.

"Easier said than done," I tell him. "Do you have a copy of this nondisclosure agreement?"

Akers says: "No. It was a formality. Some missions they asked for it, and some they didn't. On the bin Laden raid, they got it from every squad member. We assumed because of the possible political fallout."

"But they didn't give you a copy?"

He shakes his head. "We always figured the agreements were classified."

"They probably are."

"Why can't we demand a copy?" says Herman.

"Without some kind of an action pending to trigger discovery, we have no standing. Even then, if they argue national security, the court may deny access." I ask Akers if he remembers what the agreement said.

"A lot of small print," he tells me. "They dropped it on us just before we boarded the helos at Bagram. Nobody ever read the things. At the time, we figured the ticket to Abbottabad was probably one-way. Odds were the Pakistanis would bring down our choppers with missiles either coming in or going home. The fact they didn't was a miracle."

I'm shaking my head. "I'd like to help you, but at the moment, there is nothing to be done," I tell him.

"Can't we make the government either crap or get off the pot?" says Herman. "Either prosecute or leave him alone."

"Be careful what you ask for," I tell them. "You think the government wants to make an object lesson out of you? Make it clear there's a price to be paid if anybody talks on future missions?"

"That's my guess," says Akers.

"Why pick you?"

"You'd have to ask them that."

"Why not go after the SEAL who wrote the book, or the shooter who's gone public? They would seem to have more visibility."

"They also have political cover," says Akers. "A large publisher invested in the book, and a major cable channel is attached to the shooter."

"You think the Justice Department won't go after them for that reason?"

"From what I can see, the Justice Department does what it's told. A junkyard dog on a short leash held by the man in the White House and his political handlers. None of them have military experience. They don't like the military. They don't trust it. They micromanage things, interfere on missions."

"Last time I looked, he was the commander in chief," I tell him.

"It comes down from on high they want to close down Gitmo, the detention camp at Guantanamo in Cuba. What does that mean? We're not supposed to take prisoners? Instead, they want to take 'em out with drones. What if they can't? What if the risk of collateral damage is too great? What if these ECs have actionable intel?"

"ECs?" I ask.

"Enemy combatants," he says.

"Were they telling you to kill them?" I ask.

"Not in so many words. But you get the message. Keeping campaign promises to shut down Gitmo suddenly seems more important than gathering intel. It's confusing for the people in the field," says Akers.

"You're not telling me that you shot prisoners who tried to surrender?"

"No! But what if somebody says we did? All it takes is a rumor to generate international headlines."

"Are there such rumors?"

"Not that I know of," he says. "But what if there were? What then? People in Washington who were happy to drone them with Hellfire missiles will be looking for cover. Trying to scapegoat operators in the field who had to make snap judgments under fire. You know how that works. It's always bottom-feeding first. They never start at the top."

"You're not telling me that's the charge they'll bring, criminal homicide?"

"No! Absolutely not!"

"You're sure?"

"I've never shot anybody with their hands up unless they were holding a detonator and wearing a suicide vest."

"We ought to be able to do something for him," says Herman.

I check my watch.

"I hope I'm not keeping you from another appointment?" says Akers.

"Sorry. My better half is due any minute. She's in the area for a meeting. I told her I'd take her out for a drink when she was done."

"I've overstayed my welcome." Akers starts to get up from the chair. "I can pay you. I don't have much, but I can raise three, maybe four thousand . . ."

"I don't want to take your money unless we can do something for you," I tell him.

"I understand. You don't want to take the case," he says.

"If all you're worried about are the security leaks, there may not be a case. Why don't you wait and see if they bring any charges? Maybe they won't."

"In the meantime, I can't find a job. I'm thinking maybe they'll go away if I'm lawyered up," he says. "The FBI might get off my case if they know I have somebody who can complain at high enough levels to have it heard."

"Why don't we check with Harry," says Herman. "See what he says. He's in his office. Run it by him."

Herman is grasping at straws. Knowing Harry, he'll drive a stake through it. Better him than me. "If you want, I can talk to my partner."

Herman looks at Akers. He shrugs. One last appeal. Why not? "Can you do it while I wait?" says Akers. "I'd like to know before I leave the office."

"Sure."

Chapter 2

AKERS AND HERMAN wait in my office as I corner Harry, who is down the hall sitting behind his desk. I close the door but don't bother to take a seat. This won't take long. I fill him in, the rough details given to me by Akers. I'm down to the bare essentials, the retainer he's offered, when Harry finally puts his pen down and looks up at me.

"The problem is that he had to borrow money, a few thousand dollars from family and friends. For the moment, it's all he has," I tell him. "I don't want to take his last dollar. I doubt that we can help him in any event."

"You're worried about *his* last dollar? In case you haven't looked at the books lately, we're broke. We can make payroll one more month maybe, assuming you and I don't take a draw."

Times have been tough. On and off over the past two years, our practice has been shut down for the reason that

Harry, Herman, and I had been forced into hiding. A Mexican killer named Liquida, with connections to one of the drug cartels across the border, had been haunting and hunting us. By the time we came up for air, our clientele had disappeared, and our bank account was drained.

Harry is worried that if we take Akers on with a light retainer, we'll buy into the case and never see another dime. "You say he doesn't have a job?"

"And few prospects if what he says is true." Just as I say it, the door behind me opens. I turn to see Joselyn's smiling face, stylish, pixie haircut, and sparkling blue eyes as they peer at me from around the edge of the door.

"Can I come in?"

I nod. "Gimme a sec."

Joselyn slips her slender body through the partially open door and closes it behind her.

"He may be a hero, but we can't help him," says Harry. "Tell Herman no!"

"My thoughts exactly." For once, Harry and I are on the same page.

Joselyn pecks me on the cheek, and says: "Who's a hero?"

"Man down the hall," I say. "Navy SEAL says he was on the Abbottabad raid."

"Was he?"

"Apparently," I say.

"I'd love to meet him."

"No!" says Harry.

"Why not?" She turns and looks at him.

"Because we're not taking his case! Right?" Harry looks at me.

"Right."

"There's no reason we can't buy the man a drink," says Joselyn.

"That's awkward," says Harry.

"You are taking me to the Brigantine for a cocktail?" Joselyn ignores Harry and looks at me.

"Soon as I finish up here."

"Good, then the three of us can get a drink, you, me, and the hero. What's his name?"

"No!" says Harry.

"You weren't invited," says Joselyn.

Harry shoots me a frustrated expression, then drops his pen on the desk, his body language saying we've just stepped in it.

Chapter 3

SHE LOOKS UP at the waitress, and asks: "What's your recipe for Sex on the Beach?"

"I know what mine is," says Akers. "Usually starts by getting the lady drunk."

Joselyn laughs. "I wasn't asking you." She glances back at the waitress, a shapely blonde with a ponytail, packed into a shimmering black micromini dress.

We are sitting at one of the large tables at the Brigantine: Harry, Herman, Joss, Cam Akers, and I. Harry came along to protect his interests.

Akers reaches back, puts his arm around the young girl's waist, and says: "Sorry sweetheart, I couldn't resist. They don't usually let me in classy places like this."

"Now we know why," Harry whispers under his breath.

"Easy," says Herman. "Cut the man some slack."

"Give the poor girl a break," says Joselyn.

"I'd love to. From the look of the ring on her finger, she's already engaged to some worthless dude." Akers looks up and back down at the young waitress, smiling as if he's doing an appraisal, then says: "And whoever he is, he's clearly undeserving. So why don't you just give me his name, sweetheart, and I'll go break his neck for you."

"I bet you could."

"That's a bet you'd win."

She can smell the male hormones coming off him.

"Pull up a chair," he tells her.

"Love to, but I'm working," she says.

"Don't let that stop you." He tightens his hold on her. His large hand slides easily against the shimmering fabric of her dress, down toward the curve of her ass, no wasted time or motion. A move that, if most men did, it they'd get smacked seven ways from Sunday. But she just stands there weaving back and forth, smiling as if he had shot her up with morphine.

"Aren't you married," says Harry.

"Oh, ruin my day." Akers removes his arm from around the girl and sits up straight in the chair. "Just trying to have some fun."

"With two kids," says Harry.

"Now that's hitting below the belt," says Akers. "That'll cost you another shot. Make it a double, with a chaser," he says. "Make sure it's Jameson." He leans into the waitress and puts his arm around her again. "If I can't have you, then only the best will do." He glances at Harry and laughs. "You're just jealous."

"Damn right," says Harry. "The fleet's in town. Anybody with a daughter better lock 'em up."

AKERS IS OUT ahead of the rest of us, working on his third drink, the last two with chasers. He seems to have a hollow leg; it has little or no effect on him.

"The question, if I remember right, was about sex on the beach," he says.

"Not tonight," says Joselyn. "Let the poor girl go."

"The question was to you," he says.

"Me?"

"Remember? You were ordering."

"Oh, yeah. I forgot." Joselyn giggles, tries to collect herself. "They can make it straight up with vodka or use peach schnapps, as I recall."

"Peach schnapps? You don't want peach schnapps," says Akers.

"Why not?"

He leans over in his chair puts both arms around Joselyn so that she seems to disappear into his embrace, dancing dragons up to her breasts. "You want some advice?"

"I don't know. I'm afraid to ask." Joselyn looks across the table at me, wide-eyed.

"Take it straight up. Vodka. Grey Goose if they have it."

"Why?" she asks.

He says it in her ear, sensuous, his tongue nearly reaching out to touch her, just loud enough so that we can all hear him say: "A drink is like everything else in a woman's life. She wants to make sure that when she gets it—it's stiff." He glances at me, glinting even white teeth, a wicked grin behind a dark five o'clock shadow. Shades of *The Shining*, Nicholson at his most wicked. This seems to be mostly for my benefit as Joselyn ignores him. I suspect he might be reading my mind, that Harry and I have decided to decline the case though we haven't yet told him.

"I don't know . . . I was sort of leaning toward the schnapps."

"Trust me," he says.

"OK. I'll take the vodka."

"Grey Goose," says Akers. He completes the order for her.

The waitress seems reluctant to leave but finally tears herself away to get the drinks.

Akers's face is still up close to the nape of Joselyn's neck as he asks: "Are you two married?" He's an alpha male out of his cage.

At the moment, I'd like to kick him in the groin. But my leg isn't long enough to reach all the way across under the table. If I did, he'd probably break my foot.

Joselyn finally comes to her senses. She unpeels his arms from around her body. "I think perhaps you've been away in the Navy too long," she tells him.

"Me too," he says. "Look what I've been missing."

"Joselyn and I have been together for five years if that's what you're asking."

"Really? Has it been that long?" she says.

"And she's also a lawyer."

"If that's intended to scare me away, it won't work," he says.

"I don't practice any longer," she tells him.

"There, you see? So here I am swimming in a sea of lawyers, and I can't catch one." Akers tilts the business end of his bottle of brew, sucks a little into his mouth, and winks at her. "All things considered, I'd much rather hire you," he tells her.

"That's enough!" I tell him.

"Oh, shit, now I've stepped in it. Pissed you off. I guess that means you're not taking my case?" says Akers.

"That's not what he's saying." Joselyn moves around in her chair, straightening her cashmere sweater.

"That's exactly what I'm saying. Maybe we should call it a night," I tell her.

"Night?" he says. Akers checks his watch. "Not even seven bells yet. It's happy hour."

"It's late for me," says Harry. "I have to be in court in the morning."

"I don't have to be anywhere. Remember? I don't have a job."

"Maybe you should start looking again," says Harry.

"Easy for you to say."

Herman leans in and, under his breath, tells Akers maybe he should go a little easier on the juice.

"I'm not drunk. Do you think I'm drunk?" He looks at Joselyn, who doesn't answer, just smiles. "There, you see? She doesn't think I'm drunk."

"Didn't say that," says Herman. "Just want you to take it easy. That's all."

"Tell you what. Let's have a contest. See who can walk the line—blindfolded. Get some vermouth, we start a line of fire on the floor on each side, see who falls in it."

"I think we should go," I tell Joselyn.

"We just ordered drinks. Besides, you heard the man. It's not even seven bells."

"Yes, but by eight, if things keep going the way they are, he'll probably burn the place down."

Joselyn ignores me. She is enjoying herself. I can tell. Perhaps I haven't been paying enough attention to her lately. Tonight, she is reveling. Akers is just close enough to the edge to keep her entertained, while at the same time, she is safe. That and the fact that I suspect she enjoys watching my reaction. Male friction is like fireworks— exciting. It's the thing about edgy men and their volatile disposition. It attracts all women some of the time, and some women all the time. They either want to mother them, and a few even tolerate being beaten by them. They can't decide which, and nothing in between will satisfy. But I never thought this would attract Joselyn.

Harry calls it a night. He gets up, leans over the table, and says in my ear: "You know my answer." He slaps me on the back, bids everyone good evening, looks at Akers, and says: "Good luck with your life!"

"That sounds pretty final," says Akers.

Harry turns and walks.

Without missing a beat, Akers turns to Joselyn, and asks: "What type of work do you do?"

"I work for the Gideon Foundation."

"Gideon who?"

"Named after Gideon van Ry, a Dutch friend who died trying to defuse a dirty nuclear device."

"Really? For real?" Suddenly, he's serious. "Must have been quite a guy."

"He was."

"You knew him?"

"I did. But that was in another life, some years before I met Paul."

"You have quite a lady here," he tells me.

"I know. That's what I keep telling you."

"Sorry," he says. "I'm just kidding around."

I'm not sure I buy it.

"I've heard of the foundation," he tells her. "They're into nonproliferation. NGO right? Nongovernmental organization?"

Joselyn and I have been living together for about a year. I met her after she was already working for the Gideon Foundation. It is a nonprofit group that seeks to limit weapons of mass destruction as well as the latest high-tech killing machines. To Joselyn and her people, today's high-tech war toy is tomorrow's surplus war weapon, available to anyone who can pay. The aerial drones are her latest obsession. To her, they are becoming tools of assassination that may one day be unleashed on political leaders around the world.

"That's correct; we're an NGO."

"Of course, it wouldn't be the first time or the last that fissionable materials got loose."

She looks at him. "No, there have been others. I take it you have some personal knowledge?" she says.

He smiles at her. "That," he says, "would be classified."

"Of course it would," says Joselyn.

"So your foundation, what are they into? WMDs, mass destruction only, or do they range into other things?"

"We're into everything," she says.

"That's what I like. A lady who's into everything." He looks at me and grins as he says it.

"At the present time, my area of responsibility is the new generation of UAVs, the aerial drones."

"Why would you want to put a stop to those?"

"That or control them," she says.

"Why?"

"Land mines were once high-tech. Now they're buried in farm fields around the world, killing children."

"But aerial drones require infrastructure and maintenance and people who are trained to fly them. They are weapons of discrimination. You don't just bury them and forget them. Besides, they kill the bad guys."

"That depends on one's perception of who the bad guy is, which is what leads to war in the first place."

"It looks like you and I are gonna tangle," he says.

"One day, antiquated aerial drones will be flown by subnational terrorists and mercenaries. And they'll be striking targets in Western cities. You can count on it," she says. "Then what do we do?"

"You can't put the genie back in the bottle," says Akers.

"You can try."

"So you would put people like me out of work?"

"You mean the SEALs?"

He nods.

"That's not likely to happen," says Joselyn. "With the world going asymmetrical, small, highly trained tactical units are likely to remain. Whether we like it or not, you're actually part of a major growth industry."

"Was," he says. "I'm obsolete. Though I still have a few connections. Have you heard about the new generation of Tritons, the Navy's UAV?"

"I'm aware they're making changes."

"More like a whole new weapons system," he says. "How would you like to see it up close?"

Joselyn's head whips around to look at him. This is like fishing with dynamite. She would kill for the chance.

"What do you mean?"

"Some friends up north," he says. "Research being done."

"What kind of research?"

He looks at me, then leans over into her ear and whispers something.

"Really?" she says. "Where?"

"DARPA. Hunter Liggett," he says.

"You have connections there?"

Akers nods.

"I'd love to. You think they'd let me in?"

"I think they could be convinced."

"Love to what?" I ask.

She looks over, shakes her head, smiles, and turns back to Akers.

Our drinks come. Herman and I glance at each other. He leans toward me and whispers: "You gonna take the case or not?"

"There is no case." But with the bonding going on at the other side of the table, things don't look good. Harry's answer may be "no," but he doesn't have to go home with Joselyn tonight and weather her lobbying.

With one ear to their conversation, I hear her say: "Stanford research grant from the Defense Department, as I recall."

"That's where it started," he says. "But there are still some things going on there."

"Really?"

"What started?" I ask.

"Shop talk," says Joselyn. "Don't mind us." She turns back to him and continues the conversation, this time at a lower volume, whispering up close into his ear, so I can't hear.

She's not just looking for a few war stories, I suspect, but levels of detail that might surprise Akers if they get deeper into the conversation. I know Joselyn well enough. This is not just a social outing. The minute she heard about Akers, she was on a mission. I'm not worried. It has to do with work. At least that's what I tell myself.

Chapter 4

"WHY NOT TAKE his case?" Joselyn puts it to me. We are getting ready for bed. She is out of the shower, a towel wrapped around herself, her hair still wet. She is standing in the master bath, the door open, facing the mirror, tracing one of the laugh lines under her eyes with a finger.

"I'm not sure there is a case." I am seated on the edge of the bed in my underwear, looking toward the open bathroom door.

"He sounds like he needs help," she says.

"So do a lot of other people. Why do you care?"

"I just think he's an interesting man."

"That was pretty apparent."

"What do you mean?" She turns and looks at me.

"The two of you tonight."

"What about it?"

"Just that he was all over you like a cheap blanket."

"Are you jealous?" She turns and smiles at me.

"Jealous? Who me? No!"

"You sound like you're jealous."

"I'm not. It's just . . . well, in a public place like that. It's, well . . . it's unseemly, that's all."

"What are you talking about? It was a bar."

"His hands were all over you."

"You *are* jealous." She laughs. "That's OK, I think it's cute."

I feel the blood rush from my face as she looks at me, giggling. "I just think you should have stopped him," I say.

"Stopped what? You make it sound like I slept with him."

"It looked like you wanted to . . ." The instant the words pass over my lips, I know it's a mistake. I would inhale and try to suck them back, but it's too late.

"What?"

This time when I look up, there is a fierce anger in her eyes.

"Listen. I'm sorry. I didn't mean it. I . . ."

She slams the bathroom door in my face. A half second later, I hear the lock click on the inside.

"Joselyn, please!"

She fires up the hair dryer. The whining motor behind the shuttered door creates its own acoustic therapy chamber, me outside in the cold.

Chapter 5

A COUPLE OF days go by. It is getting lonely sleeping downstairs on the couch. I tell Harry this, and he asks: "So what are you gonna do?"

"I don't know. She is out of town overnight on business. She left me a note this morning."

"A note?" says Harry. "It's that serious?"

"I tried to call her a couple of times on her cell. She is not taking my calls. I'm hoping that by tomorrow, when she comes back, she'll be in a better mood."

"Never been married myself," says Harry. "But my experience with women tells me that's not likely to happen. With them, silence is like a sliver under the skin. It tends to fester."

"How can I talk to her if she won't take my calls?"

"Buy her some flowers," says Harry.

"You think so?"

"I don't know. Like I say, I've never been married.

What did you finally tell Akers?" Harry changes the subject. "Did you tell him we weren't taking his case?"

"I didn't tell him anything. He never called back."

"That's strange," says Harry. "He wanted an answer that day. Remember? He seemed pretty desperate for counsel."

"Maybe he found somebody else," I tell him.

"What is Herman saying? Is he taking it lying down? He was the one in Akers's corner. He and your better half," says Harry. He rubs it in.

"He says Akers hasn't shown up at the gym since our meeting at the Brigantine. He hasn't seen him. Said he tried to call him. There was no answer."

"Tell him to leave the man alone. We don't want to kick a sleeping dog."

"You think flowers might work?" I ask him.

"You might try sending her some. Find out where she is staying tonight and have them delivered," says Harry. "Or if that doesn't work, try some diamonds."

"I'll start with flowers."

"Cheap screw," he says.

For a man with no real love life, Harry sometimes has good instincts.

I call Joselyn's office and ask her secretary where she is, the name of the hotel where she is staying. What I get back is not what I want to hear. According to her secretary, Joselyn is not away on business. She has taken time off from work. They are not sure exactly how long she'll be gone. What is worse, they have no idea where she is.

When I tell Harry this, he looks up at me. "Maybe she just needed some time off to be alone." But even Harry is not buying this. I can tell by the look in his eye as he says it.

Call it paranoia, but the specter of Joselyn and Akers off together is beginning to do a number on my head.

Chapter 6

AKERS'S EYES WERE shaded behind a badass pair of Gatorz sunglasses, his gaze riveted on the highway as they sped north up I-5.

"Nice car," said Joselyn.

"Yes, it is."

He was driving a gleaming black Escalade. It looked new, clean inside and out as if it were uninhabited, unlike Joselyn's old Honda, which was a rolling trash can. She wondered how he could afford it.

"Have you had it long?"

"What?"

"The car," said Joselyn.

"Not long. No. You know, I was a little surprised when you called," he said.

"You did invite me."

"I didn't say I was unhappy. Just surprised."

"Why is that?"

"I figured it would take you a little longer to get away."

"You mean my job?"

"I mean your boyfriend," said Akers.

"Paul, yes, well . . . sometimes he thinks he owns me. He doesn't."

"I was glad when you called," said Akers. "I needed to get out of town. I was just looking for an excuse to leave, for a place to go and someone to go with."

"Wanderlust?" she asked.

"You might say that. So when you called, it was perfect. Did you tell Madriani where we were going?"

"No."

"So I take it he doesn't know you're with me?"

"He doesn't need to know," said Joselyn.

"Why, because he'll go ballistic?"

"That's his problem. As far as I'm concerned, this is business. My job."

People at the foundation had heard all kinds of stories about the latest incarnation of the Triton, the Navy's latest version of its high-altitude long-range UAV. The problem was that none of the information could be verified. They could wait until *Jane's US Military Aircraft Recognition Guide* published specs, but that could take years. The craft was rumored to be modified for STAL, short takeoff and landing, and to have a beefed-up undercarriage and larger wheels. Speculation was that it was being designed to land in a remote location and take off again. Why wasn't clear. One possible theory was rescue missions, assuming the soldier or downed airman could move to the vehicle and get on board, perhaps in some kind of a pressurized capsule. Word was it was be equipped with fine computer controls for midair refueling. Given the Triton's current capacity to stay aloft for more than a day, in-flight refueling could mean that it might stay in the air almost indefinitely. The ability to hover over a battlefield for hours or even days and to provide real-time surveillance and intelligence would be a huge breakthrough. And then there were the sci-fi stories regarding ordnance, optics, and radar. It was believed to possess not only ground-penetrating radar, but a new system that would allow radar visuals inside hardened military structures. How this was achieved wasn't clear, but Joselyn suspected that it was the development of this system that led to a civilian police counterpart. Police agencies around the country had begun deploying handheld radar systems that could penetrate walls to observe human conduct, movement, and activity inside homes. They had done this with little or no public notice and no assurance that search warrants would be obtained. Such systems could shred the entire concept of any reasonable expectation of privacy anywhere or under any circumstances. If such a system was about to be deployed in the skies, Joselyn wanted to know about it. And she wanted to be the first to broadcast the alarm.

"Sounds like the two of you had an argument."

"What?"

"You and Madriani."

"Maybe."

"I hope it was about me."

"Let's drop it," said Joselyn.

"Whatever you say." Akers looked over at her and smiled.

"How long do you think it will take us to get there?" she asked.

"Six hours, maybe less depending on traffic. But we got a late start. I was thinking maybe we'd stop somewhere along the way for the night. It would be best if we get there in the early morning."

"Why is that?"

"That'd be our best shot to see the bird on the ground," he said.

"Are you sure it'll be there?"

"As far as I know. I talked to one of the researchers on the phone night before last. They're testing takeoff and landing in the morning."

"STAL," said Joselyn.

"How would you know about that?" he asked.

"What you in the Navy call scuttlebutt," she told him. "Do you go up there often?"

"Hunter Liggett?"

She nodded.

"No. Not these days anyway."

Fort Hunter Liggett is situated on the eastern slope of the coastal range in central California. It was part of the old Mexican land grant known as Rancho Piedra Blanca. The grant was issued to the Pico family by the Mexican government in the 1840s. In 1865, George Hearst, then a prosperous mining engineer and soon to be U.S. senator from California, bought the old Rancho as part of his holdings, hundreds of thousands of acres spanning from

San Simeon on the Pacific Coast to the old Mission near San Miguel, on what is today Highway 101. Hearst's son, William Randolph of publishing fame, sold large portions of the ranch to the federal government in 1940, just before the outbreak of World War II. Two military installations were established, Hunter Liggett and Camp Roberts, both of which remain in operation today. They run from dry grasslands under ancient oak trees to rugged mountains and serve as training grounds for tank crews, gunnery operations, and, at times, classified aerial operations. Thirty years ago, a military security blanket was thrown over large portions of the ranch when a highly classified fighter-bomber crashed there during testing. Though the government hushed it up, and the public wouldn't hear the term for years, the aircraft in question was an early version of the stealth bomber.

"Any truth to the rumor that there's a spook facility of some kind up there?" asked Joselyn.

"What do you mean ghosts?"

"You know what I mean. CIA," said Joselyn.

"Ah. The Culinary Institute of America."

"You can't talk about it, is that it?"

"I think they offer cooking classes at the mess from time to time."

"Forget I mentioned it."

"I used to get up there regularly. To the airfield at Liggett, I mean," he said, changing the subject. "Back then, it was one of my assignments. I did tech surveillance, so I got involved with the first primitive birds. You know, the little hand-launched radio-controlled jobs. The

UAVs that look like toy models. I got into it just as they were being developed. We field-tested some of the early prototypes."

"On actual missions?" she asked.

He nodded.

"That was before SOC, Special Operations Command, settled on the Puma. It's been through three incarnations now. I think they're working on another. Are you familiar with it? The Puma?"

"A little bit," she said. "These early toys topped out at five hundred feet, fifteen-kilometer range, three-and-a-half-hour battery, optical and infrared cameras . . ."

"You do your homework, don't you?"

"I figured I'd better read up on what the Navy uses. I didn't want to waste your time."

"Waste away," said Akers. He looked over at her and smiled. "It's amazing how far they've come in terms of range, altitude, and optics. You can read the name stitched on a guy's tunic from five hundred feet up. Nobody can hear the thing. Feeds all the data to a command center through a satellite. Real-time surveillance. You can keep it in the air for two hours to be safe, bring it back, charge it up, and send it out again. When you're done, you could fold it up and put it in your backpack."

"It is amazing," said Joselyn. "Now all we need is to find some peaceful applications."

"Oh, we found those," said Akers.

"You have?"

"Yeah. If you search and kill enough of the right people, the result is peace."

"Search and rescue is what I was thinking," said Joselyn. "The fact is, there is nowhere you can have privacy anymore."

"From me you mean?"

"No. I mean from your UAVs. Nowhere to hide."

"I suppose that's true."

"Why would you want to hide from me?"

"I don't know, but I'm sure you'll give me a reason." Joselyn winks at him. "Are you sure these friends of yours will allow me in? I mean, if this is classified stuff . . ."

"If it's guys from Stanford, civilian researchers, don't worry about it. Let me do the talking. If there are military types around, then we'll have to be more careful. I'll take the lead."

"I don't want to get you in any trouble," said Joselyn. "Don't worry. If anybody goes to jail, it's probably gonna be you."

"Well, that makes me feel better."

Chapter 7

HERMAN HAS BEEN trying to reach Akers on his cell
phone for two days without success. I am having the
same luck with Joselyn. In her note, she didn't say when
she would be back, only that she had some business out of
town. I thought she would be home by now. But there is
no word. I am beginning to harbor some serious worries.

Eight o'clock in the evening, and I'm out of the house,
on the hunt for leads as to where she might be and
whether she is with Akers. I leave a note, large block letters on the kitchen table in case she comes home. I tell her
to "PLEASE CALL ME!"

Herman and I visit a bar and grill on Orange Avenue
about a block and a half north of the law office. It's a place
called McP's. According to Herman, it's a hangout for
some of the SEALs down on the Strand, not the BUD/S
trainees but older, enlisted types. Herman had met Akers
there twice for beer in the evenings. He tells me that Cam

has friends who frequent the place. Herman has met a few of them. I'm hoping that one of them might know where Akers is so that I can contact him to find out if Joselyn is with him, and if so, to make sure she's OK.

My suspicions are not grounded in sand. I know Joselyn. I picked up enough of the arcing energy between them on the other side of the table that evening at the Brigantine to know that it wasn't just sexual dynamism at work. Neither was it idle curiosity or hero worship. Jocelyn was on a quest, looking for information, the reason she wanted to meet Akers in the first place.

Joss reads *Jane's Defence Weekly* the way most women read *Vogue*. To her, a SEAL from Team Six, somebody who had been to Abbottabad, would be a walking repository of military secrets. There would be no end to the dark, tactical deeds and technical details such a person would know.

There was talk that night about drones, UAVs, unmanned aerial vehicles. That much I heard, and more. It was one of Joselyn's relentless quests—the black-box doings and dealings of DARPA, an acronym in search of a name—the Defense Advanced Research Projects Agency. I had heard her talk about it enough times that it was now committed to memory. DARPA is the Pentagon's equivalent of the stiff-upper-lipped Q in James Bond. If the military needs a new toy, DARPA will invent and develop it. Or it will contract with a university research lab to do the job.

The minute Joselyn mentioned the foundation where she worked, Akers had used DARPA like a lure. He cast it into the narrowing abyss between then. And when Joss bit, he reeled her in. The question is, did they go off together, and if so, where? If it's work she is doing, then that's fine. I had, after all, left her alone enough times for my own career that she has every right to do the same. If it is more than that, I need to know. Right now, I am worried.

When we get to McP's, I know the place. I have passed it a thousand times walking here and there, but for some reason I have never gone in. It's not what I would think of as rowdy dive for hard-bitten SEALs. It looks more like a tourist spot.

There are small-paned windows underscored by glossy, green-painted flower boxes across the front. From the outside, the building has a quaint cottage feel. There is an oversized cupola perched on the roof ridge, a boxy ornament that looks as if it's about to swallow the building. Four large windows in the cupola emit a green glow from inside. This is topped by a dome.

Inside, it's cozy, what you might call warm. There are six or eight stools against the bar at the far end, a few tables and booths against one wall with green, tuck-and-rolled curving benches to match the green carpet. You get the sense that if you looked hard enough, you might see leprechauns peering out from the potted plants against the wall.

Herman scans the bar, four guys perched on the stools talking. One of them is tall. They seem very fit. They could be SEALs, but I don't know.

Herman shakes his head. He doesn't recognize any

of them. He checks the tables and studies a small group gathered in one of the booths. They look like tourists. "No luck," he says.

I'm about to turn and leave when he grabs me by the arm. "Let's look outside."

We troop through the place. I follow Herman. We head for the open door at the back, what looks like a small beer garden, wooden tables under large umbrellas. As we exit the building, I can see that the patio outside is bigger than I thought. Several long strings of incandescent lights illuminate the area, giving it a party atmosphere.

"I think I recognize one of them," says Herman.

Before I can turn to look, he walks toward one of the tables. "Hey, how you doin'?" Herman is smiling, big and broad. It's hard to miss a man who is built like a mountain, black, bald, shiny dome and all.

Three young guys are sitting at the table, none of them smiling. You get the sense there is something clannish in the gathering.

"You remember me? Met you the other day. I was with Cam Akers."

"Oh, yeah! Yeah, I remember. Your name's, ahh . . ."

"Herman."

"That's right. How you doin'? Why don't you pull up a chair and join us?" The guy talking is eyeing me as I draw up behind Herman. "Who's your friend?"

"Name's Paul," I tell him.

"How you doin'?" Still seated, he holds out a hand.

I shake it. He has a grip that feels like a vise. He nearly crushes my knuckles before he gives the hand back to me.

"Actually, we're lookin' for Cam," says Herman. "You haven't seen him, have you?"

The guy shakes his head, looks at his companions. Now there's a chorus of shaking heads. "No, haven't seen him for several days now."

One of the other guys says: "He comes and goes. Leaves town every so often. May not see him for a week or more. Since he rotated out, he's become sort of a ghost, if you know what I mean."

"Not exactly," I tell him.

"No place to belong," he says. "Sort of floats, here, there. Feel sorry for him. Don't tell him I said that."

"Of course not," I say.

"He's a good man. Good SEAL. Lot of service," he says. "It's a tough situation."

"Do you know him well?" I ask.

"I know him."

"He came to my office, said he needed a lawyer. I'd like to talk to him again if I could." I figure if I keep them talking, maybe I'll learn where I can find him.

The three of them look at each other. The one Herman knows finally looks up at me and says: "Why would he need a lawyer?"

"I'm not at liberty to say," I tell him. "But I would like to talk to him."

"He's not talkin' that second-man shit again, is he?"

"What shit is that?" says Herman.

"That he was the second man up the stairs at Abbottabad. That he's the one who actually shot bin Laden." The guy looks at me as he says it.

"No. Nothing like that," I say.

"Good," he says. "You just want to be careful. You go talkin' that shit, you get yourself killed."

"How's that?" I ask.

"Crazies out there. Lone wolves or worse. You start talking like that, one of them might come lookin' for you. Word is Akers may have blabbed to the media that he was the one who pulled the trigger. I told him that was dangerous. Shouldn't do it."

I am thinking this is how Akers got himself in trouble with the brass.

"Was he the second man?" I ask.

"Says he was. But who knows? I wasn't there. Another guy says he's actually the one. He's been all over the airwaves with it. Conventional wisdom, for what it's worth, says he's the shooter, not Akers. But then, this man's aware of the other claims."

"Other claims?"

"By Akers and one or two others." The guy shrugs. "Who knows what really went down? The shooter didn't seem to take offense from what I heard. Passed it all off as the fog of war. People see different things, believe what they want to believe. You ask me," he says, "I'd want to remain the unknown sailor."

I laugh. "That's great." I stand there feeling as if I've been punched in the stomach, staring out into the darkness beyond the lighted patio. Cam Akers may have made himself a prized target for some crazed lunatic out there, and for all I know, at this moment he might be riding in a car with Joselyn sitting right next to him.

Chapter 8

"TELL ME," SAID Joselyn. "No beating around the bush. No happy-horseshit military hype. What was it really like at Abbottabad?" They were back in the car, early morning. They spent the night in a seedy little motel at a wide spot in the road called Buttonwillow.

"Like any other mission," said Akers.

"Really?"

"Only more so if you know what I mean."

"No. Tell me?"

"We knew it was important the minute they called us in. It was like your dad calling you in to tell you he has a present for you, busting out with smiles, big fucking box shaped like a bicycle in the middle of the floor, but he won't tell you what's in it. Minute we saw the mock-up in North Carolina of the actual compound, we knew. Why take all the time to build this mock-up unless the man inside is pretty damn important. And that's a short list. Any one of us would have given odds at Vegas it was UBL. Of course, we didn't know for sure until later in Afghanistan."

"But what was it really like?" said Joselyn.

"It was more intense. We knew the stakes were high. They were taking a chance flying us in without approval from the Pakistan government. We all knew that ISI, Pakistani Intelligence, was riddled with leaks. If they found out about the raid, the compound would be empty by the time we got there. We were willing to take the risk. I was! I think we all were. Anybody wanted out, there were a hundred other SEALs waiting to take his place. They would have jumped at the chance to go. How many operations do you get like this in a lifetime? One, maybe? It's like being on the beach at D-Day. You might get killed, but you don't want to miss the party. It's what you do. It's why you tolerate all the training, take all the pain. Once the action starts, you pretty much go on autopilot. You do your job. It's over so fast, sometimes you have trouble remembering parts of it. That's when it goes good. When everything works out right. You hope you don't get killed, or worse, screw up and kill somebody else. The difficult parts are before and after. Waiting to go in can be nerve-racking. Lot of things going through your head. The only thing worse is thinking about it afterwards."

"Why is that?" she asked.

"When things don't go well," said Akers. "You can't go back and change them."

"Because it's over," said Joselyn.

"It's never over."

"Maybe we shouldn't talk about it," she said.

"You can't understand unless you've been there," said Akers. "You see your friends go down. People you've been with for years. You know their families, their wives. Your kids play with their kids. You're like brothers, then suddenly they're gone. Sometimes you ask yourself 'did I do something wrong'? You always try to tell yourself no. But you're never sure. And there's nothing you can do about it. You're helpless. Do you know what it is to be helpless?"

"I don't know. I'm not sure."

"All the fucking training in the world is useless. But the worst part—the worst times are when you're free. When you've got nothing to do. That's when the devil comes visiting," said Akers.

"You mean when you're off duty?"

"No. I mean when you're done. When they've used you up, turned you out," said Akers. "That's when you sit around thinking. Because there is nothing else to do. As long as you have another mission, you're fine. You're busy. Your mind is focused on trying to survive, trying to keep your friends alive. It's when they take that away from you, that's when you descend into hell. It's the random nature of all of it that drives you crazy. You wonder why them and not you? Why did they have to die? Why do I deserve to live?"

"You can't think that way," said Joselyn.

"Oh, yes, you can."

"Is that why you got out? Left the Navy?"

"I don't know. Some of the guys used to do the Clint Eastwood thing. Remember the movie, the Western, the line before he blows the guy's head off . . . 'deserve's got nothing to do with it.' But he was wrong," said Akers. "Deserve has everything to do with it. A foot this way, a yard that way with a bullet or a hot piece of shrapnel makes all the difference in the world."

"You're not God," said Joselyn. "You can't change fate or the fact that a bullet and another man shared the same space at the same time. That's physics."

"Is that what it is?"

Joselyn looked over at him. He was gripping the steering wheel with both hands, animated, muscled arms flexed as if he might rip the steering column from the firewall of the car by its roots. A rivulet of a tear ran down his cheek from under the dark glasses. She couldn't see his eyes.

"I didn't mean to raise subjects that are painful," said Joselyn.

"From my experience, there's not a whole lot in life that doesn't come with some kind of pain."

"It's been that bad?"

"At times. But they tell me it's good to talk about it."

"Who's 'they'?"

"People. Friends. You know."

"Maybe we need to find something happier to talk about," said Joselyn.

"Agreed."

Akers took one hand off the wheel, settled back into the seat, and relaxed a little. He glanced into the rearview mirror, then goosed the accelerator until the speedometer reached seventy-five, where he set the cruise control.

As the car settled in, open road and empty lanes, he said: "You know, I find it very easy to talk to you."

"I'm glad."

He reached over and put his hand on her thigh. "You're a very nice lady."

She picked it up by one finger and handed it back to him. "And you're married, and I'm in a relationship," said Joselyn. "Let's not forget that."

"Where's your sense of adventure?" he smiled.

Joselyn took out her sunglasses, saw they were smudged, and exhaled on the lenses. She looked about for something to wipe them with. Seeing nothing, she reached forward to open the glove box to see if there was some Kleenex. Instead, what she saw inside was an Avis rental-car envelope with the contract sticking out of it. "You didn't rent the car?"

He looked over, saw the open glove box, and quickly reached across to slap it closed.

"There was no need to spend the money on a rental." Joselyn knew he was out of work and probably short of cash.

"My car wasn't up to the trip—pretty beat-up," he told her.

"We could have taken mine," she said.

"My party. I invited you. It's all right. Don't worry about it," he told her.

"At least let me pay for it," said Joselyn.

"NO!" The way that he said it, the tone in his voice made it clear this was not negotiable.

"Then I'm buying lunch, and dinner," she told him.

"And gas. I have an expense account, and this is business. Remember? The foundation. You're doing me a favor, so please let me help."

"You are," he said. "You're here. That's a big help. I enjoy your company."

"And I yours. But that's not the point. This is costing you money."

"I don't mind. In fact, I'm enjoying it. Tonight we can save a little by sharing a suite," he said.

"I'll be paying for my own room tonight, just like last night. I thought that was understood. That was the deal."

"Don't get angry. It'll give you a chance to cheat," said Akers.

"What do you mean, cheat?" Joselyn shot him a look to kill.

"On your expense account." He turned and smiled. "What did you think I meant?"

She took a deep breath. "Let's talk about something else."

"Sure. Whatever you want."

"Let's talk about your wife. What's she like? What's her name? I don't think you've told me."

The question dissolved the smile from his face.

"Allyson."

"What's she like? Tell me about her."

Akers didn't respond. He just sat there, hand on the wheel, eyes forward.

"And your children. You have two kids, right?"

"Correct."

"Tell me about your family."

He nibbled a bit on his upper lip, put his other hand back on the wheel, and said: "Sore subject. Don't really want to talk about it if you don't mind."

"That's fine."

Akers reached over, turned on the radio, and plugged his cell phone into the receiver on the console. He pushed a few buttons until a sound track came on. It was edgy music, loud enough that the vibration of the base reached inside Joselyn's rib cage and rattled her.

Chapter 9

"TOLD ME THEY had no choice but to let him go," says Herman.

"Did they say why?" I ask.

"No." Herman is talking about the Orange County Sheriff's Office. He called a contact, someone he knows inside the department and checked Akers's story out regarding his job, the reason he was fired.

We talk as I drive. Herman and I are headed to Akers's house, trying to find his wife. Maybe she knows where he is.

"My guy couldn't say much. Being it's a personnel matter. If he says too much, or the wrong thing, he could lose his job. But he did confirm that the FBI had contacted them about Akers. Wouldn't say way, not in so many words, but it's pretty clear," says Herman.

"What's that?"

"Cam's been working his mouth," he says. "What the

guys at 'McP's' told us last night, that Akers claimed to be the shooter, second man up the stairs. Think about it. The FBI comes knocking, making inquiries. If Akers made himself a target for some Muslim-warrior wannabe, the sheriff's gotta have serious concerns about the danger this poses to other personnel. Say nothing of the public. Then think of the liability if he knows about it, and the department gets sued cuz somebody got killed or seriously hurt."

None of this makes me any more comfortable with the thought that Joselyn, at this moment, may be with him. "So now you're thinking your buddy is a loose cannon?"

"Sorry I brought him to your office. What can I say?"

"You didn't know."

"Let's assume for the moment she's not with him," says Herman. "Where else would she go? Any thoughts?"

I shake my head. I was on the phone late last night and early this morning calling her relatives, all the ones I know, her sister, her mother, and a cousin who lives up in L.A. I didn't want to worry them, so I told them she left town on the spur of the moment without telling me where she was going, and I need to reach her. I told them her phone must be on the blink. They hadn't seen or heard from her. The same with her friends. It's not like her. She would call somebody unless there was a reason. And the only reason I can think of is that she's with Akers and doesn't want to discuss it with anyone.

"You're working yourself into a hole on this," says Herman.

"I don't know what else to do."

Chapter 10

AKERS FINALLY TURNED off the music in the car and asked Joselyn: "How'd you sleep?"

"You mean except for the trucks rolling through town all night and the occasional bedbug chewing on my leg?"

Buttonwillow sported an Olympic-class truck stop, two small motels, and an oasis of gas stations. Miss it, and you might not get where you're going. Highway Five through the Central Valley was an octane desert and had been since its completion in the late 1970s. There were long stretches between gas stations and even fewer places to eat.

"I warned you. You should have slept with me. I'd have protected you from the bugs, and my bite's not that bad."

Joselyn didn't ask him how he slept because she knew. Twice during the night, he woke her up shouting in his sleep from the next room. The place had thin walls, but even if it had been solid concrete, she would have heard him. Then in the morning, on the way to the car, he turned back. He forgot something. He went back inside his room. Through the open door, Joselyn saw him lift the pillow off his bed and grab an unsheathed knife, a heavy seven-inch blade, what the military called a Ka-Bar. He slipped it into his backpack. She wondered if he was carrying a gun.

"How about tonight maybe we share a room?" he said.

"You don't quit, do you?"

"No, and you want to know the truth? I don't think you want me to." He looked over at her and gave her a full dental set, pearly whites. He hadn't shaved. The forest of even dark stubble gave his face a more rugged appearance if that was possible. "Quit, that is."

"If it makes you happy, you go on thinking that," said Joselyn.

"I will."

"If anybody ever accuses you of lacking self-esteem, you just send them to me. I'll set them straight," she told him.

"Thank you."

"It wasn't a compliment," she said. "Does the ego come with the turf?"

"What do you mean?"

"I mean people who deal in death on a daily basis, dishing it out and risking it, sooner or later I suppose must develop a fairly strong God complex."

"So you think I look like Apollo?"

She gave him a smirk. "Tell me, what does it feel like to kill someone?"

"Do you have anyone specific in mind?"

"Stop it!"

"I mean, if you and Madriani had a fight, I can take care of him for you." He was smiling.

"Seriously, I'd just like to know. How do you deal with it?"

"I knew this was coming."

"What?"

"Analysis," he said. "Are you a pro or is this amateur hour? If you're a pro, I want to see your head-shrinking license."

"So you prefer not to talk about it," said Joselyn.

"As long as the right people get killed, I don't have any problem with it."

"Some people get off on it," said Joselyn.

"Some people might. I don't. It's a job. Has to be done."

"How may people have you killed?"

"Today? None." He looked over at her and grinned. "But then the day is young."

"You know what I mean. Over the course of your career? Do you know? Any idea of the number? Or do you just do what they say, shoot 'em and let God sort it out?"

"I thought you said *I* was God."

"You see, you just keep avoiding the question. I think you have a problem."

"Tell you the truth, I don't keep a tally in my head. The notches were all carved on my carbine, but I turned that in. So I'd have to check my computer and get back to you on the number," he told her. "Fair to say there were days when I probably overshot my limit. But then, it's not like fishing, is it? Can't really catch and release after you've pulled the trigger."

"I imagine it helps to be cavalier about it," said Joselyn. "OK, so tell me, when you do it, are you usually up close, or are you far away? I suspect it's probably easier to kill them when they're at a distance. Less personal. "

"Dwarfs and pigmies I shoot up close cuz they're smaller and harder to hit," said Akers.

Joselyn, who was trying to remain serious, couldn't help but smile.

"Sometimes up close, sometimes far away. It depends on the situation," he said, "that and how quickly they're trying to kill you or one of your friends."

"Do you just look 'em in the eye and pull the trigger?"

"I'm beginning to feel like a bug under glass," he told her.

"Does it bother you to talk about it?"

"Not if it excites you. In that case, I'm happy to discuss it."

"That's not why I'm asking."

"I think it is. You know what I think?"

"I don't think I want to know."

"I think you get off on being with a man who's killed for a living."

"That's nonsense. I don't! That's not true."

"Now who's being defensive? So let me ask you, does it repel you?" he said.

"I didn't say that."

"Well, there you go. You're just sort of neutral on the

subject, is that it? That means with a little training, you could probably learn to kill with the best. You and I could go on the road, do a revival as Bonnie and Clyde."

"Why is it you can't be serious?" asked Joselyn.

"I guess it's just not in my nature."

"Is it that, or is it just that it hurts too much to talk?"

"Who says?"

"I don't know. I'm asking."

"What is it with you? I want to talk about us. And all you want to talk about is me."

"There is no us," said Joselyn. "This is business. And besides, I've never met a member of DEVGRU, so I'm curious."

"You don't mind if I crawl off the slide and out from under the microscope."

"Sorry, I didn't mean to pry."

"You know, you're a strange gal," he said.

"How is that?"

"Well, for most women, half the fun is being pursued, but that doesn't seem to hold true for you."

"Maybe it's just that rutting season is over," she told him.

"That's not what I meant."

"I know what you meant."

"You and Madriani, is that it?" said Akers.

"Yes. I suppose."

"What is it he has that makes you happy?" asked Akers.

"What it always is between two people."

"Lust?" said Akers.

"That lasts a nanosecond," she told him. "There's always a physical side, but it's the comfort level that counts. When we're together, I feel like I'm home if that makes any sense. Do you know what I mean?" She looked over at him.

The expression on his face was not one of understanding. To Joselyn, it looked more like fear, as if he had no clue. She wondered what it must be like to be at such a loss.

"You share the same values I suppose. Two bleeding hearts?" he said.

"Oh, God, no," said Joselyn. "We argue all the time about politics. It's like pounding sand. I'm a progressive. Paul's a Neanderthal. We gave up on that long ago."

"Maybe I misjudged your other half," he said.

"Yeah, the two of you would probably get along."

"Yesterday you asked me about the CIA. Let me tell you, the old CIA used to keep things in check, making sure that the right people got shot so that the wrong people didn't get into power in some bad places around the world. Now you folks, you progressives have waved on the Arab Spring. We come to find out this eruption of democracy is nothing but an exchange of tyrants. Getting rid of those who were once friendly to Uncle Sam in favor of those who are not. Excuse me for saying, but this is what love-in liberals always produce. Don't get me wrong, I've got nothing against love." He winked at her. "But spineless policy always makes the world a more dangerous place. The thought that if we just love everybody, they'll love us back, is how you get raped. That and the thought that if it doesn't work, you can just bullshit your way through. After all, our fearless leader knows this always works with the voters. The problem is that, for the most part, they're fucking morons," said Akers. "So when things get out of control, he's gotta call in the masked man."

"I suppose that's you on a white horse," said Joselyn.

"Hi Ho Silver!" said Akers.

They rode on in silence for about an hour, then turned west toward 101. Akers occasionally looked over to check her out, a lusty glint in his eye. Joselyn's shapely legs, one draped over the other, outlined in skintight stretch pants, left little to the imagination.

An hour later, they were speeding north up 101, cutting through the military base, what was left of Camp Roberts, now a National Guard training post. A few miles farther on, they came to a sign on the road: FORT HUNTER LIGGETT.

The sun was an hour into the sky to the east as they approached the guardhouse. Akers stopped the Escalade at the Army checkpoint, rolled down the window, and told the MP: "We're registered at the Hacienda."

The guard took a look at Akers's driver's license, made a note, checked the license plate on the car, wrote it down, and waved them through.

"What's the Hacienda?" asked Jocelyn.

"Hearst's old hunting lodge. Military uses it for guests, but it's open to the public. You'll like it. No bedbugs. Least I don't think so." Moments later, they pulled up in front of a sprawling Spanish Colonial building, gleaming white walls in the morning sun, red-tile roof with a tower.

"Are you sure they're open?" Theirs was the only car in the parking lot.

"Yep. Best time of the year, off-season. Got the place to ourselves. Let's go register and check in. We can unload the car and head over to the airfield," he told her. Akers stepped out and went to the back of the car and opened the rear door. Inside was a large ice chest the size of a footlocker.

"What's that?" she asked.

"Food and supplies," he told her.

"We're not staying for the month," she said.

"Never can tell," said Akers. "And you always want to be prepared."

"No, really," she asked.

"It's food. In case you haven't noticed, we're in the middle of nowhere. The nearest restaurant and grocery is over a half hour away. Up to King City. I hope you can cook, cuz I can't boil water."

Joselyn wasn't looking forward to setting up house-keeping with him, one hand on the frying pan, the other trying to ward him off.

He started to pull the chest out of the back of the car. "Got some steaks for tonight. We can barbecue 'em. Hearst used to have the servants bring food over from the ranch house."

"Where's that?" asked Joselyn.

"Over there. Other side of those mountains." Akers nodded toward the Santa Lucia Range in the distance to the west. "State owns it now. William Randolph hated the fuckin' name, Hearst Castle. Insisted they call it the ranch. Now that's a man with a healthy God complex. Unfortunately, he's not here to entertain us. Get the back door," he told her.

She closed the back door, then grabbed her overnight pack from the backseat, closed that door, and followed him toward to the lodge. "Aren't you going to lock the car?"

"Who's gonna steal anything out here. If the snakes don't get 'em, the fucking MPs will probably shoot 'em out of pure boredom. Only action they're ever gonna see."

Akers lugged the ice chest into the building. Inside was a large, rustic reception area and a desk with a clerk behind it. The place was dated but clean and beautiful. Like a time capsule, it looked as if it hadn't been touched since Hearst's last visit.

Akers put the ice chest down on the ancient floor. He wrote his name on a slip of paper and handed it to the clerk, who pulled up the reservation.

"It's already paid for on a credit card," said the clerk.

"I know. We're in the tower suite. I don't imagine you have somebody who can bring up our luggage?"

"Leave it, we'll take care of it," said the clerk.

"Separate rooms," said Joselyn, "remember?"

"You're worse than a nun," said Akers. "Not to worry, there are two bedrooms in the suite."

The clerk handed him the key. "If you like, I can show you the way."

"No need. Been here before." Akers grabbed Joselyn by the hand and almost jerked her off her feet. She was still looking around, up at the beamed ceiling, what money could build. "Wait 'til you see the colonnade out back," he told her. "You'll feel right at home. Think you're in a nunnery."

"You could fit an army in this place," said Joselyn.

"At times they do. Brass abuses the hell out of the place entertaining themselves. Used to hunt in the hills for wild boar," said Akers. "Don't know if they still do or not."

They climbed the stairs, got to the top, and Akers opened the door, turned, and said: "Would you like me to carry you over the threshold?"

She smiled and brushed past him into the room. It was the size of a large condo, windows looking out at the gardens at the back of the building. Manicured grounds, green grass and boxed hedges. "It's very nice."

"And romantic," said Akers. "Very romantic. There are two bottles of champagne in the ice chest. You cook a candlelit dinner, and I'll get you drunk and do the rest."

She walked over and glanced in the bedrooms. "Which room do you want?" she asked.

"Don't know. Let me check the beds."

Joselyn walked over to survey the kitchen. A few seconds later, Akers came out of one of the bedrooms and went into the other. A quick appraisal, and he came back out. He was holding a small pocketknife in his hand, cleaning his nails.

"What's your verdict?" she asked.

"Why don't we wait, and we can draw straws later for sleeping arrangements," he told her. "First, let's go take care of business. Let's get to the airfield before we miss the bird. They're liable to fly it out of here to Palmdale or Edwards before we can take a gander."

Joselyn certainly didn't want that to happen.

They headed back to the car. As Akers pulled out of the lot, he turned and headed north.

"I thought the airfield was the other way."

"It is," he said. "First, I want to show you something." He turned left onto a side road, then right and went north for about a half mile. They pulled into a parking lot in front of sprawling old adobe. It was covered by Spanish tile, its red color bleached to a rusted hue by two centuries of scorching sunlight. There were two crosses on top, a smaller one on the outer sculpted facade in front, and another larger one at the peak of the main building behind it.

"It's an old mission," said Joselyn. "What's it doing on a military base?"

"San Antonio de Padua," said Akers. "Most people never see it because it's inside the guard post. They assume they can't get to it. It's open to the public, they just don't know it. And the Army doesn't advertise it."

"It's beautiful."

"According to experts, it's probably the most authentic because of the pristine setting. The land around it hasn't changed much since the old friars and conquistadors whipped the Indians to build it. That was in the late 1700s," he said.

"I wish I had my camera."

"We can come back later, you can get some pictures if you like."

"Thank you," she said. Joselyn turned and smiled at him. "There is a softer side to you after all. You need to show it more."

"Stick with me, sweetheart, and I will." He leaned over, kissed her on the cheek. Strange as it seemed, even to her, Joselyn didn't move or make any effort to pull away.

They headed to the airfield, a heliport on the western perimeter of the base. Akers drove the Escalade into a dirt parking area that bordered the tarmac. Several large military helicopters were parked out on the asphalt apron. Between them was a small van. Beyond that, out on the shortened helipad runway, was a large, sleek UAV. Joselyn could see that it was good-sized and jet-powered.

IT LOOKED LIKE nothing so much as a giant white porpoise, a bulbous head up forward where the camera's optics, infrared, radar, and other surveillance systems were arrayed. It had two long, slender, glider-like wings reminiscent of the old U-2 spy plane, and a v-shaped tail. On top, near the aft section, was a single large jet intake. The craft was sleek, curving, and had very few sharp angles. To Joselyn it looked as if it might possesses cloaking or stealth properties once airborne. Her attention was fixed on the underside of the nose of the UAV, looking for anything that might suggest a new system of home or structural invasive radar.

"It looks bigger than the Triton," she said.

"It is," said Akers. "Long-distance, high-altitude, and with STAL capabilities. Short takeoff and landing. Best part is, it can stay in the air over a target four times longer than anything we currently have. And can carry a full complement of ordnance."

"I'd like to take a closer look," she said.

"Sure, gimme a minute." He reached into the backseat and pulled a pair of field glasses from the floor. He quickly scanned the area around the runway near the UAV. There were three men standing near the aircraft. "I know two of them. Third one I don't recognize," he said. He noticed another vehicle next to it in a dirt lot. It was a small light blue sedan with federal-government license plates, and lettering on the door: FOR OFFICIAL USE ONLY. "Somebody else is here, but I can't be sure who it is. Let's go ahead, take a chance. Just follow my lead," he told her.

Joselyn opened her door and got out. She was anxious to get up close. A photo, even if she had to snap it with her cell phone, would have been priceless The legal penalties for such activity could also put her in prison for espionage. She didn't dare. Not unless they gave her permission. She knew there was little hope of that. There was no question the UAV was highly classified.

Akers put the glasses down and opened his door. Just as he did it, he looked in the rearview mirror and saw a Humvee with two MPs drive onto the dirt parking area at a good clip. They pulled up behind him in a cloud of dust. Before he could get out of car, one of the MPs was already moving toward his door. The other one walked quickly toward Joselyn, who was already outside.

"Ma'am, get back in the car," the MP told her.

The other one looked at Akers through the open door. "Sir, may I ask what you're doing here?"

"Can I get my ID?" said Akers.

"Go ahead."

Akers pulled out his wallet, opened it, and slipped a heavy plastic ID from the inside. He handed it to the MP, who looked at it, studied it for a second, looked at Akers's face, and said: "Sorry, sir. Didn't mean to hassle you." He handed the card back to Akers. "Who's your friend?"

"She's with me. I'll take full responsibility," he told the kid.

"Yes, sir. No problem." He saluted Akers. "Have a nice day." The MP looked at his partner, and they both headed back to the Humvee.

As soon as they pulled away, Joselyn, her hands shaking, turned to Akers, and said: "I was sure they were going to arrest us. How did you do that? That wasn't your driver's license you gave him."

"No."

"What was it?"

"My SEAL ID from DEVGRU," he said.

"I don't understand. You are out of the military."

"Yes, but I never turned in the card," he said.

"How did you do that?"

"Told them it was lost."

"What if he had checked? Called in your name," said Joselyn.

"He didn't."

"But what if he had?"

"I knew he wouldn't."

"Why?"

"Alpha principal," said Akers. "Kid stationed out here. I doubt he's ever seen action. Minute he sees that card, he knows I swim in it. He can sniff my ass, but that's as close as he wants to get. Now he can go back to the mess, tell his three buddies and the cook how he met somebody from Team Six."

"So you're a celebrity," said Joselyn.

"If you want to call it that. Like it or not, I made his day. Hell, a kid stuck out here who has to drive for an hour to catch a movie, I probably made his whole year," said Akers.

"You do like the edge, don't you?"

"Gives me a rush," he said. "Seems like the only thing that keeps me alive. Let's go take a look at this bird."

Chapter 11

HERMAN AND I finally find Akers's house. It's a small, ranch-style bungalow on a quiet side street in Chula Vista. The yard looks as if it has hasn't been mowed or watered in a couple of years. Dead palm fronds from a tree next door litter the front of the house. There is a weathered FOR RENT sign, its red lettering faded to pink, wired to the chain-link fence along the sidewalk.

"Are you sure this is it?"

"It's the right address," says Herman.

I park at the curb, turn off the engine, and we get out. We make our way through the gate out front, close it behind us, and walk ten feet to the front porch. There are a few children's toys stacked up in one corner next to a small bicycle and a skateboard with one of the wheels off.

Herman tries the doorbell. We hear it ring inside, a single quick "ding-dong" and what sounds like a dog barking somewhere way off in the distance. We stand there waiting. There is no sound from inside. Herman punches the button again, and we wait. "Looks like no-body's home."

I look out from the porch across the front of the house. The attached garage is at the end of a short driveway out-side the chain-link fence on the right side as you face the house from the street.

"Let's see if there's a car inside," I say.

We head out through the gate. Herman goes down the driveway and tries the garage door, but it's locked. He looks along the side of the garage for a window, but there isn't one. "Wanna go around the back, take a look?"

Just as he says it, a woman comes out of the house next door. "Are you looking for Allyson?"

She is kind of frumpy, heavyset, with dishwater-blond hair dried-up and frizzed out by enough bleach that it looks as if it's been struck by lightning.

"We're looking for Mrs. Akers," I tell her.

"She's not home," says the woman.

"Do you know when she'll be back?"

She shakes her head. "No. Have no idea where she went." The woman makes her way slowly from her front porch across the lawn to where I'm standing in the drive-way. "Her kids didn't show up at the school bus stop today or yesterday. It's right across the street. I can see it out my front window. No one's been around for a couple of days. Usually, Allyson calls if she's going away. Sometimes she has me watch their dog. But she must have taken it with her. I'm Joanna Boggs." She holds out her hand. I take it and shake it.

"And you are?" she says.

"I'm Paul."

"Does Paul have a last name?" she asks.

"Madriani."

"Thank you. Very melodious," she says. "I'm thinking she probably went up to see her sister. Lives up north somewhere. Could've taken the kids and the dog with her. She's done that before."

"Have you seen Mr. Akers?"

"No. I haven't seen him around for quite a while. Last time was right after they moved in."

"But he lives here, right?" I ask.

She shakes her head. "Not that I know of. He hasn't been around for, I'd say at least two months now."

"You mean they're separated?"

"Can I ask what your business is?" she says.

"I'm a lawyer. I have some business with Mr. Akers."

"Is he in trouble?"

"Not that I know of. You wouldn't happen to know where he lives?"

"Can't help you there."

"When did they break up?" I ask.

"I don't know how much I should tell you. Are you his lawyer?"

"Not exactly. I just need to talk to him, that's all."

"Can I ask what it's about?" she says.

"It's confidential."

"I see. Well, like I say, I probably shouldn't say anything, but they were having some troubles. Young couple. It's a shame," she says. "Allyson is a real nice girl. And the two kids, Cam Jr. is eight and little Jamie is gonna be six in another month or so. Cute kids. Real nice. I don't know all the details, and I really probably shouldn't be telling you this, but Allyson, I think, has had just about enough."

"Enough of what?" I ask.

"I think it's his job. I don't know exactly what type of work he does. Her husband, I mean. She wouldn't tell me. I know he was gone a lot. But whatever it is, it's dangerous."

"How do you know that?"

"About two months ago, she told me she thought some people were after him, trying to kill him. I'm thinking maybe he's into drugs or something. You know, the border being this close and all. She told him to stay away from the house. When he wouldn't listen, she got a lawyer and went to court. I told her she was doin' the right thing."

"You mean she filed for divorce?"

"No. At least I don't think so. God only knows why not," she says. "She got a piece of paper says that he can't come near the house."

"A restraining order."

"Yeah, I think that's what she called it. He can't see her or the kids without special permission, and he has to stay clear of the house. I'm sure that's why he's not around."

"That would probably do it," says Herman.

"She was very worried. I think she loves him. But what are you gonna do? She's got the two kids. She's gotta protect them."

"You don't happen to have a phone number for her?"

"I tried her cell phone, but there's no answer, and her voice mail isn't set up. You know how you get that message every time you call?"

"Yeah, I hate that," says Herman. "She's lucky to have a neighbor like you." He glances at me, a sly smile passing across his lips.

"I feel sorry for her," she says. "I do what I can."

I pull a business card from my wallet and hand it to her. "Listen, will you do me a favor? If you see her or hear from her, can you give me a call at that number? I'd like to talk to her if I could."

"Sure." She looks at my card. "If I hear from her, I'll let you know." She smiles pleasantly and heads back to her house. Herman and I turn and walk toward the car.

"It's a good thing we weren't looking to whack him," says Herman. "With a neighbor like that, you wouldn't need to set up surveillance. Ask her nicely, she'd probably shoot him from her kitchen window for you."

"Why don't you check the courthouse and see if you can find the file, any information on the application for the restraining order," I tell him. "We need to find out what the hell's going on."

Chapter 12

AKERS SHOOK HANDS with two of the men standing near the large UAV. One of them was a Stanford researcher he had worked with on other visits. The other was from Grumman, the aircraft manufacturer. The third man he didn't know. There were smiles all around.

Joselyn couldn't hear everything said because of the persistent, high-pitched whistle from the craft's idling jet engine. If they kicked it up, she would have to plug her ears or lose her hearing.

Cam kibitzed around for a few seconds until the guy from Stanford introduced him to the third man. Joselyn edged in closer, trying to hear.

"Charlie here's from Langley. He's out visiting."

"I take it you're the money?" said Akers.

"Part of it," said the man.

"Good to meet you. My name's Cam." Akers held out his hand.

The other guy hesitated.

"He's OK," said one of the other guys. "He's with DEVGRU."

"Ah!" The mystery man loosened up. "Good to meet you. I'm Chuck Henley." They shook hands. Henley was tall and lean, about six foot two, a shock of short, sandy-colored hair that stood up on top of his head like a stiff-bristled brush. He wore tan slacks, a red polo shirt, and a light blue windbreaker zipped about halfway up his chest, as if he might lose the thing later in the day when it turned warm.

Joselyn was surprised how many people didn't know that Akers was out of the military. But then, as she thought about it, it made sense. Unless the military sent out some kind of an all-points memo, how would people know? He'd been out only a short time, a few months. It would take a while for word of mouth to get around.

"Who's your friend?" Henley looked over Akers's shoulder.

"I'm Joselyn." She reached out and took his hand.

"She's a friend," said Akers. "We were out for a ride heading up the coast, thought we'd stop by. You don't mind, do you?"

"You're here now. So I suppose it doesn't matter. Just don't take any pictures," he told them.

"How is she doin'? Have you seen her in flight?" Akers turned the question toward one of his friends from Stanford.

"Had her up yesterday, testing out some of the avionics, shook out some of the bugs," said the guy. "Sent her down to Palmdale, from there over to Edwards and back. Climbs right up to altitude. Gonna have to send her back to Palmdale tomorrow for some maintenance."

"We're working off a list of fixes," said the man. "But she's coming along nicely. Some programming stuff. The usual glitches." He looked toward the guy from Grumman, and said: "Why don't we cut the engine and check it out?"

The other man turned toward the van parked out on the apron not far from one of the helicopters. There was a small dish-antenna array on the roof. He made a gesture—the fingers of one hand drawn across his throat. A few seconds later, the drone's jet engine began to die. It took a few more seconds, then went silent. Joselyn could finally hear clearly again.

"Well, we know that works," said Akers.

"Let's hope we don't have to use it when it's airborne," said Henley. "From what I can see, the glide ratio on this one's not great. I don't want to have to call home and tell 'em they just lost a billion in R&D against a hillside in California."

"I take it your background is Air Force?" said Akers.

"Who else would the 'Company' hire to monitor this beast?" said Henley.

The CIA recruited from all of the military branches, depending on the expertise they needed. They recruited regularly from DEVGRU, turning SEAL operators into field agents in battle theaters and elsewhere.

"So I take it you're the project manager?" said Akers.

"Guilty," said Henley.

"Lemme guess; you're over budget and past delivery date?"

"That doesn't take a crystal ball," said the man from the CIA.

"You flying it out of there?" Akers gestured with his head toward the parked van.

"For the time being. But I'm trying to get them to move flight control to one of the hangars over at Moffit, so we can give it a more thorough test."

"We're getting there," said the guy from Stanford. "Just give us a little more time. You can't rush these things."

"Oh, you can," said the Grumman man, "it's just the results may not be pretty." He motioned with his hand like a plane flying into the ground.

Joselyn looked toward the engine mounted in the rear. It looked similar to the Triton and the Global Hawk. She assumed it was the same power plant, a single large fan-jet. What looked different were vents underneath the fuselage, what appeared to be rotating nozzles, probably directional jet exhausts that would give the vehicle lift on takeoff for short runways. She wanted to ask, but she didn't dare. If she could see it take off, she would know.

"Excuse me." The Grumman man moved toward a closed compartment at the rear of the drone. She moved aside to let him get by.

Joselyn already had a list in her mind of at least a dozen questions, the first being about radar. But she knew that if she asked, the man named Henley would give her the third degree, want to know what she was doing here before he handed her over to the MPs. Better to play the dumb date. In the meantime, she glanced toward the underside of the UAV at the nose, the round ball turret with its various lenses and data-gathering gizmos. The radar was not likely to be there. Assuming it functioned in the traditional way, it was more likely to be housed inside the fuselage behind a protective dome, either in the porpoise-like nose or the underbelly.

"Don't let us get in your way," said Akers. He motioned for Joselyn so that they could move to the other side of the aircraft, where they might get a better look and get away from Henley.

As soon as they were out of sight, Henley started talking to the Stanford engineer. "I don't mind the SEALs, but I wish they'd keep their frog hogs at home," he said.

"What's a frog hog?" whispered Joselyn.

"Shhh!" Akers didn't want to tell her it was a term used to describe a female SEAL groupie.

"Who is he?" said Henley. "Guy didn't give me a last name."

"That's Akers. I told you about him. He helped us a lot in the early going, some of the early craft with field tests. Guy that went to Abbottabad.

"That was Cam Akers?"

"Yeah. I thought you knew."

"I know the name. I heard he got wounded. Something about a medical discharge."

"Apparently not," said the man from Stanford.

Akers leaned into Joselyn's ear, and whispered: "I think we better go. Come back tomorrow. Maybe he'll be gone."

Joselyn didn't want to leave. She wanted to see the thing fly. But Akers had her by the arm, with a grip that was cutting off circulation.

They went around the back of the aircraft this time. Joselyn could tell that Akers didn't want to talk to Henley anymore.

When they cleared the v-shaped tail fin at the rear of the drone, the guy from Stanford looked over and saw them. "Cam," he said. "You didn't take a wound on a recent mission, did you?"

"No. That's a rumor goin' around. Don't know who started it, but if I find him, I'm gonna kick his ass," said Akers. "Listen, we gotta run."

Henley turned and looked at him. "Good to meet you. You too, miss. Have nice ride up the coast."

"Where are you staying?" asked Akers.

"Here on the base," said Henley. "Place called the Hacienda."

The sigh from Akers was palpable. Joselyn could feel the hot exhaust as it came out his nose.

"How long you gonna be around?" asked Cam.

"Not sure yet. Why do you ask?"

"Just wondering. Take care. Have a good flight back." Akers and Joselyn moved toward the car. "That cuts it," he said.

"Cuts what?" she asked.

"Never mind. Tell you about it later," he said.

Chapter 13

Back at the office, in our conference room that doubles as a law library, Harry, Herman, and I are brainstorming where we go next. Without some lead, we are helpless to figure out where Joselyn and Akers might have gone. We can't even be sure they're together. But if not, where is she?

Herman has struck out on the latest information, the court file regarding the restraining order on Akers keeping him away from the family home.

"I talked to the clerk," says Herman, "but he couldn't find the file."

"Why not?" says Harry.

"They tell me the US Attorney's Office intervened in the state-court proceedings. They obtained a federal court order sealing the file."

"On what authority?" I ask.

"They cited a section of federal law," says Herman. He hands Harry a slip of paper with a number on it. Harry gets up from the table and goes to the stack of books behind his chair. A few seconds later, he is back with one of the volumes. He looks up the section, then he flips a bunch of pages and checks the title. "It's part of the Patriot Act, national security," says Harry.

"Why would they do that?" I ask.

"Have to assume there was something in the file, perhaps something said during the hearing, they didn't want made public," says Herman.

"Could have been something in the wife's petition. Especially if Akers had been talking up details of his missions," says Harry. "Think about it. She's under the gun. She's afraid he's gonna end up saying something that draws some fanatic lone wolf to their front door bent on revenge. The petition could be loaded with details the government didn't want out there."

"Who represented Akers on the Order to Show Cause?" I ask. Maybe I can call the lawyer and find out what's going on.

"Without the file, we have no way of knowing," says Herman.

I pull out my cell phone. When all else fails. I try calling the landline at my house, hoping that Joselyn will pick up. Instead, it rolls over to voice mail. I hang up and check the messages. There are two, neither of them from Joss. I try her cell phone. It rolls over immediately and goes right to her voice mail. There's no answer.

Herman looks at me. I shake my head. He is also on his phone, listens for a moment, then pushes the button on the screen and hangs up. "What'd you get?"

"Her phone is either turned off or outside the service area," I tell him.

"Same here," he says. "Don't want to bust your balloon, but I'm guessing she's with Akers. Otherwise, one of them would have answered by now."

I get out of the chair and go to the computer in the corner of the room, take a seat in front of the screen, and move the mouse until it flickers on. I remember Akers and Joselyn that evening at the Brigantine. In between jibes over Sex on the Beach, they talked about UAVs, unmanned aerial vehicles. Only a weapons groupie like Joss and a constant commando like Akers could get it on talking drones over drinks. One of them, I can't remember which, had mentioned something about DARPA and Stanford.

I punch up Google and plug in some terms: *UAVs, DARPA, Stanford.* When the page pops up, I look at the sites, but nothing sets off any bells. I hit the image button at the top of the screen. Among the pictures is one that catches my eye. The words *Stanford researchers . . .*" appear in the abbreviated cut line beneath the picture. I open the image. It shows a man in civilian clothes working with an early UAV, a primitive, boxy, handheld toy model you could probably pick up today for a few hundred bucks at any hobby shop. But this was back then.

I click on the VISIT PAGE button. When it opens I read the article to get more information and there, in the middle of the piece, are the words: "Fort Hunter Liggett Army Garrison in California." And I remember. Akers had his tongue halfway into Joselyn's right ear when she asked him: "Where?" His answer was Hunter Liggett.

I turn to Harry and Herman and ask if either of them have ever been there.

"Passed the sign a hundred times," says Harry. "It's up off 101 somewhere north of San Luis Obispo."

"Isn't that Camp Roberts?" said Herman.

"As I recall, they're a few miles apart," I tell them. "Nothing else there. A lot of open country, away from the coast."

"You're thinking that's where they are?" says Herman.

"You sure the place is still open?" asks Harry. "I thought it got caught up in the base closures a few years back and was shut down."

I type in "Fort Hunter Liggett, California." Sure enough, at the top of the list is an official Army website. I open it. "It shows as an active training site according to this. A hundred and sixty-five thousand acres. The only dirt landing strip for C-17s in the US. IED training, as well as training for allied nations. I'd say they're open for business."

"What makes you think they're there?" says Harry.

"Because Akers used it to lure Joselyn away the night at the Brigantine. It's where they developed some of the early drones. From what I gather, they're still using some of the facilities. To Joselyn, that's like shooting her up with meth. Tell her there's classified military weaponry on display, something the Gideon Foundation hasn't yet seen, and that you can get her into the show. Akers becomes the Pied Piper."

"I think you got a hard-on for this guy," says Herman.

"I admit I don't like him."

"I wouldn't either if I thought he was out there some-where with my woman," says Herman. "Sorry I said that. I'm even sorrier I brought him by the office."

"Too late now," says Harry.

Herman looks at him, and says: "Paul's taking it better than you are. You'd think it was your better half."

"I'm my own better half," says Harry.

"How far away is this place?" says Herman.

I check the mileage on Google maps. "If we leave now, we could be there late tonight," I tell him. "Says six and a half hours from San Diego to Hunter Liggett."

"Is there some way to make a phone call?" says Harry. "Save yourself a trip. Somebody we can call, to see if they're there?"

"Who?" I ask.

"I don't know," he says.

I look at the website again. There is a general infor-mation number. I call it. When they pick up, I ask the male military voice on the other end whether he can tell me if a former Navy SEAL by the name of Cameron Akers has checked in on the base. He tells me to hold a second. When he comes back he wants to know who's calling. I lie. I identify myself and tell him I'm Akers's lawyer and that I need to talk to him. He tells me that no one by that name shows up on the current roster. He says they don't get the morning roster 'til later in the day.

I think for a moment, then I tell him. "He's meet-ing with some researchers. They're working on a drone system up there. . . ."

"Oh, yeah. Those guys are over at the heliport. I can connect you."

I look at Harry and smile. A few seconds later, I hear the call as it is ringing through. It's answered by a PFC. I don't catch his last name. I run Akers's name by him.

"Nobody here by that name," he says. "But he might be outside."

"Can you check for me?"

"Sorry, I can't leave the desk," he says. "I can take a message. If he shows up, I'll give it to him."

I think for a moment. Then I tell him I'll call back later. Akers is not likely to return a call based on a message from me. And if he finds out I've located them, he's likely to come up with some other lure to take Joselyn on another adventure."

"Are they there?" says Harry.

"I think so. Can't be sure," I tell him. "But given what I know, if I had to guess, I'd say yes. Can you hold down the fort?" I ask Harry.

"Would it matter if I said no?"

"No," I tell him.

"Get the hell out of here." He smiles. "Go find her. We all know you're not going to be worth a damn until you do."

I grab my coat. Herman gets his. One of the secretaries asks where we're going as we race for the exit.

"Talk to Harry," I tell her.

"When you gonna be back?" Harry yells from the library.

"Tomorrow!" I tell him. Herman and I are out the

door before Harry can ask any more questions. We get to the parking area behind the building. I head for my sedan.

"You wanna drive?" says Herman.

"Thought I would."

"Then gimme a sec. Gotta get something out of my car."

It was a good thing I didn't bring the old Jeep today. Herman heads to his Buick. He pops the trunk and fishes around for something inside. When his hands come out, he's holding a pistol in his right hand, what I know to be his compact .45 auto. As he moves toward my car, I see him check the loaded clip. He slides it into the grip of the pistol and slaps it home. He doesn't pull the slide to chamber the first round. Herman is careful with firearms.

When he gets into the car, I ask him: "Do you really think we're gonna need that?"

"You never know. But better me than you" he says. "Feeling the way you do, you'd probably empty the clip into Akers the second he says hello."

Chapter 14

JOANNA BOGGS STOOD at her kitchen sink, doing the dishes and looking out the window at Allyson Akers's backyard. She hadn't seen hide nor hair of her neighbor or her children in three days. She was beginning to worry, wondering where they were or why they hadn't come home or at least called.

She looked down for a moment at the dishes in the sink, looked up, and said: "What in the world?" She reached up with a wet hand and flexed the venetian blinds to get a better look. Boggs thought she glimpsed something moving in the yard next door. Whatever it was had disappeared down below the bushes that ran along the other side of the fence separating Boggs's property from Allyson's backyard.

She watched for a few seconds, then realized that she wasn't imagining things. Some of the low branches on one of the bushes were moving. She glanced down to rinse some suds off a plate, and when she looked back up, there it was, standing in the middle of the yard, scratching its paws on the grass as if it had just taken a dump.

"Gypsy!" Maybe they came home, thought Boggs.

The small ball of fuzz was perched on four tiny legs that moved with the speed of bristles on a sonic toothbrush. Before Boggs could dry her hands and head for the door, the mutt had disappeared through the doggie hatch and back inside Allyson Akers's house.

Boggs was anxious to find out where they'd been. She headed out her front door, across the lawn onto Akers' porch, and rang the doorbell. She waited, but there was no answer. She rang it again. Still nothing. She tried to peek through one of the windows but couldn't see anything. It was dark inside. The afternoon sun was hitting the front of the house, creating glare on the glass.

She went out through the front gate, turned, and looked back at the house. She walked up the driveway and tried the garage door. It was locked. They never locked the garage door when they were home. But if they hadn't come home, what was the dog doing in the house? Something was wrong. Boggs knew it.

If Allyson and the kids had gone away overnight, they would have either taken the dog with them or asked Joanna to watch it. Gypsy was a pound pup. The two kids had fallen in love the minute they laid eyes on her. Allyson had no idea as to its breed or the precise pollution of its gene pool. She called it a "rat-terrier," saying it was a cross between the two.

Boggs walked along the side of the garage, unlatched

the chain-link gate that led to the backyard, and closed it behind her. She tried the back door, but it was locked. She looked through the glass window that formed the top panel of the door. This looked in on the service porch. She could see through to the open kitchen door, but there was no one there.

She bent over and pushed the neoprene flap that sealed the doggie door until it opened a little. She held it there. "Heeere, Gypsy, come on. Come see Joanna. Come see Grandma." She made some kissing sounds, rattled the door, and waited, then did it again.

After a few more seconds, a blond, furry ball showed up at the opening. Its delicate pink tongue darted through the wild bouffant of fur that covered its entire body. The dog's tongue licked Boggs's fingers with all the fury of a butterfly having an orgasm. Joanna reached inside, scooped the animal up in one hand, and straightened herself up. "What are you doing here all alone?"

She cradled the small mop of wiggling hair close to her bosom and continued talking to it as if the animal might talk back. "Did they abandon you? We're gonna have to talk to them when they get back, huh? Yes, we are."

She continued to clutch the dog as she took another look through the glass in the top of the door. She saw nothing out of the ordinary, except one thing. An old washing machine, dented and peppered with pits of rust stood against the wall. On top of it was a pile of dirty clothes waiting to be washed.

The open wicker hamper was empty, as if Allyson had been called away in the middle of her chores. Maybe they left in a hurry, she thought. Perhaps a family emergency.

"How's my baby?" She looked back at the dog. "I think you need some food. You come with me."

She headed through the side gate around the front, across the lawn, and back to her own house. Boggs didn't put the dog down until she closed and locked the front door behind her. She went into the kitchen, grabbed a large handful of kibble from a bag in the cupboard under the sink, put it in a small bowl, and placed the bowl on the kitchen floor.

Before she could turn to get some cheese to put on top of the kibble, she heard the crunching as the dog's tiny teeth went to work gnawing at the contents in the bowl. This wasn't like Gypsy. Usually, you had to force-feed her. Joanna realized that the animal hadn't eaten in days.

She wasn't sure what to do. But she knew something was wrong. She couldn't call the police. What could she tell them? Dog abandonment. First-degree dirty clothes. They'd think she was crazy. She put a little mild grated cheddar on top of the kibble and watched the dog as it chowed down, devouring the soft cheese. She filled another bowl with water and put it on the floor next to the food.

As she stood up to put the cheese back in the fridge, Boggs saw the business card on the counter where she had left it earlier that morning. She picked it up and looked at the name—Paul Madriani. They had at least shown interest, the two men, the lawyer and his much larger African-American friend. She thought about it, then laid the card back down on the countertop. If she overreacted and did something foolish, Allyson might get angry. Joanna could lose a friend or worse, contact with the children she loved. That would be stupid. She glanced down at the dog. The cheese on top was gone, as was most of the kibble. If Gypsy kept eating like this, she would consume half her body weight. She watched the dog for a few minutes. It started acting really strange. It wouldn't settle down. It scratched at the back door, then went to the front door and did the same. She figured it needed to relieve itself. She opened the backdoor and let the dog out. What happened next sent her into a tither.

Chapter 15

HERMAN AND I seem to skim up over the Grapevine,
into the Tehachapis, and on toward the Central Valley.
Herman has convinced me that taking I-5 and cutting
west near Bakersfield will save time. If speed is any in-
dication, he is right. My gaze constantly checking on the
rearview mirror, I set the cruise control at seventy-five
and settle in.

Comfort comes in the form of other cars passing us
like shooting stars. It's the opposite of swimming with
sharks. I don't have to be the slowest one on the road, just
slower than you. Sure enough, a few miles on we pass one
of these galactic starships. It is stopped at the side of the
road, a black-and-white with its colored flashing strobes
parked behind him, the cop at the driver's side window
taking his pledge to help retire the state debt.

According to Herman, we are about an hour south of
the turnoff, the connector to 101. He keeps checking the

GPS on his spanking-new cell phone. He tells me the cell signal keeps cutting in and out as we traverse the mountain pass. For the moment, he has three bars. "Where do you think they might be staying, assuming they're in the area?" Herman is talking about Joselyn and Akers.

I have grappled with the abstractions of whereabouts and well-being, where she is, and whether she's all right. I have tried to corral any other anxieties. Call it denial, a defense mechanism. Any angst beyond the immediate will have to struggle for existence in that subterranean part of my brain where ancient reptilian roots have expelled reason. Even at my most paranoid, I have difficulty imagining Joselyn sleeping with him. I tell myself this. The question is do I believe it? I do my best. I try to soar above the yawning chasm of distrust, only to find myself sucked into downdrafts of doubt. The question is, do we ever really know anyone? We all like to think so. The raw nerve begins to throb.

"There's not much there," says Herman.

For a second, I think he's reading my mind, until he says: "Not many places to stay until you go north to King City about a half hour farther up the road. Except there's one," he says. "Place called the Hacienda. It has a historical note," he tells me. Herman is reading to me off the 3G. Or is it four now? I can never keep it straight. He tells me he's getting a booming cell signal as we head down the long, steep ramp at the north end of the Grapevine, out of the foothills, and onto the Valley floor. Everything he reads is going in one ear and out the other, my mind wandering.

"According to this, it says it's located on the base, but it's open to the public."

"What is?" I ask.

"The Hacienda. Haven't you been listening? You think I'm readin' this small print for my pleasure?" says Herman. "I'm gettin' a headache. Pay attention!"

"Sorry," I tell him. "If you think they might be there, we should check it out."

"If they're staying in the area near the reservation, I don't see a lot of other places they could be. Like I say, unless they went up to King City. It's possible, but I don't think they'd do that if they got business on the base. And this place, the Hacienda, it's not that expensive."

"Is there a phone number?" I ask.

He squints at the screen on the phone and runs his finger up and down it, looking. "Yeah. Here it is. You want me to call 'em? See if they're checked in?"

"No, not yet. Let's get closer before we do it."

"Why? You thinkin' they might rabbit?"

"Not them, him. If we talk to the desk, and they mention it to Akers, unless I miss my bet, he's gonna find some other place to take her, some other hot news flash for the foundation. Let's wait 'til we're on top of them."

"I'm wondering," he says. "Look at my phone."

I glance over. "What about it?"

"I got five bars," he says. "I can't get five bars in my apartment back in Diego."

"So?"

"If I'm gettin' five bars, and if they're up this way, why can't we reach Joselyn or Akers on their cell phones?"

"Good question."

"Unless they're turned off," he says. He looks over at me. "You know what I'm getting at?"

"You're thinking maybe they don't want to be disturbed."

"I don't know," he says. "Far be it for me . . ."

"Maybe we're busting in on a love nest." I take my eyes off the road to glance at him. I read his mind.

"Don't get angry. I don't want you to misunderstand what I'm sayin'." Herman won't look me in the eye. He just keeps talking. "I know you and Joselyn been together a long time," he says.

"It's an awkward situation for all of us," I tell him. "You're afraid, and so is Harry. None of us can be sure how this is gonna end. If you say the wrong thing, question Joselyn's commitment, you're afraid you run the risk that if she and I get back together, you're on the outs. By the same token, you want me to know you've got my back. You don't have to say anything more. I understand. Stepping in front of me to take a bullet is one thing. Mopping up tears and dealing with a blubbering, heartbroken lover is beyond your call of duty."

"Didn't say that."

"You don't have to," I tell him. "No need to be afraid. If it happens, we'll find a good bar and tie one on. Go on an Olympic-class bender and leave Harry holding the bag of bones that was our practice."

At least it is brave talk. I suppose we'll have to wait and see if it happens, and if so, whether it holds up.

Chapter 16

AT THE HACIENDA, Akers decided not to park the Escalade in the lot out in front. Instead, he pulled across an unpaved area, drove between two old oak trees, circled around the tennis court, and brought the car to a stop in a cloud of dust in a service area behind the Hacienda.

Joselyn looked at him. "Why are we parking here?"

"Wouldn't do to have Henley see the car out in front when he comes back to his room tonight," he told her. "He saw us get in and drive away, so he knows our car. He thinks we're moving on up the coast. He sees us here, booked in a room, he's gonna start asking questions again. Man's got a lot of curiosity," said Akers.

"Why all the deception?" asked Joselyn.

"As I explained, if there was any brass around, we'd have to be careful. The only reason we're allowed in is because they think I'm still with DEVGRU."

"I'm not comfortable with any of this," she told him.

"You're the one who wanted to come."

"To be candid, I'm not sure I would have had I known you were going to lie to everyone."

"Why? Just because they don't know I've separated from the Navy? That's their problem."

"It's more than that and you know it. Using a false ID, lying to the military about having lost it."

"There's nothing false about the ID. It's mine," he said. "Here, you want to see the picture on it, I'll show you." He started to reach for his wallet.

"Don't bother. You know what I mean."

"Come on, let's not sit here and argue." Akers got out of the car and closed the door. He left Joselyn sitting in the passenger seat, fuming. Finally, she got out and followed him back toward the Hacienda.

"How long are we going to stay here?" she asked.

"Long as it takes," said Akers. "Stick with me and we can probably get you some pictures of that bird out there. Just think, you bring those back to your precious foundation, they'll probably give you a big gold star."

"And get indicted for espionage? No thanks," she said. "I think I've seen all I need to see."

"What about the radar? You wanted to find out about that."

"If it's up inside under a dome, I'll never see it. And even if I did, I'd have no idea how it functions."

"So you want to cut and run, is that it?"

"I need to get back to San Diego," said Joselyn. The fact was that Akers's conduct had begun to unnerve her.

"Why, so you can go running back to Madriani?"

"What business is that of yours?"

"I just don't think you're ever gonna be happy there, that's all."

"What would you know about it? You don't know me, and you don't know Paul."

"If you were happy with him, why did you come with me? And don't tell me it was to go drone-watching."

"Is that what you think?"

"Paramount evasion of the insecure," said Akers "is to answer a question with a question."

To Joselyn, these words coming from Akers's mouth seemed out of character. It sounded more like something he might have picked up in a therapy session. She was starting to get a picture in her mind, and it wasn't pretty. Screaming in the night. The knife under the pillow. The abrupt fashion in which he pulled her away from the airfield the minute Henley mentioned rumors of a medical problem.

Inside the Hacienda, Akers handed her the room key and told her to go on ahead up to the room. He would join her in a minute. There was something he needed to take care of.

Joselyn turned and walked toward the stairs. She stopped a few feet away around a corner where he couldn't see her and listened as Akers talked to the clerk behind the desk. "I have a friend staying here. His name is Henley, can you tell me which room he's in?"

"Mr. Henley is in one of the arcade rooms," said the clerk. "I'm sorry, but it's our policy not to give out room numbers. But you can reach him on the house phone in your room. Just give the operator his name."

"Thanks."

The words *house phone* hit Joselyn like a thunderbolt. She turned and ran quickly toward the stairs. She scrambled up them two at a time. Why, if he was trying to hide from the man, would he want Henley's room number? She made a mental note that Henley was staying in the arcade. This must have been the area Akers referred to as the colonnade, a long, covered walkway bordered by guest rooms on one side and open, mission-style arches on the other. From what Joselyn had seen, there were two arcades, one in the back looking out on the gardens and the other facing the parking area out front.

She was breathless by the time she got to the room. She used the key, opened the door, and quickly closed it behind her. Then she ran to the phone. It was on a table in the living room. There might be extensions in the bedrooms, but she didn't have time to look. She picked up the receiver and pressed zero. The hotel operator came on the line.

"How can I help you?"

"How do I make a long-distance call?"

"Would you like to bill it to your room?"

"Yes."

"You can either dial it yourself or . . ."

There was a knock at the door.

"Never mind." said Joselyn. "I'll place it later." She hung up, then tried to collect herself, paused for a moment to catch her breath, then walked calmly toward the door and opened it.

Akers came in and closed it behind him.

"Did you get your business taken care of?" she asked.

"Yeah."

"Didn't take long," she said.

"I wanted to buy some gum, but they don't have any," he told her.

"I think I have some in my purse. Would you like me to take a look?"

"Don't bother," he told her. "The urge has passed. Maybe later."

"So what do you want to do?" she asked.

"I'll give you three guesses," he said. "The first two don't count."

"I don't want to just sit around and waste the whole day," she said.

"Sitting wasn't what I had in mind," he said. "I thought we'd just stay here and relax."

The gleam in his eye told her this was code for "let's stick around so I can jump your bones." The thought of having to fight him off here in the tower, where no one could hear her if she yelled out, didn't seem a good tactical choice to Joselyn.

"So what you're saying is we can't finish what we came here to do until Henley leaves, is that it?"

"I can." He winked at her, reached out, and put his hands around her waist. "But I don't know about you."

"As far as I'm concerned, I've seen everything I came to see."

She smiled, looked away as if she were embarrassed. She hoped it sold, that he didn't feel her trembling. "You did a great job. I got up close, took a good look. I mean, it's true I didn't get information on technical specs. But I never thought I would. The fact is, you've been a big help. We'll do it again sometime. I couldn't have gotten near it without you. You really are sweet. Some lady is very lucky to have you."

The second she looked him in the eye, Joselyn knew it was one lie too many. He dropped his hand from her waist and stepped back. The smile faded from his lips.

"Calm down," he told her. "You don't need to be scared. You think I'm gonna hurt you?"

"No!" Her voice went up three octaves. "That's not what I was thinking at all."

"You sure?"

"Yes. It's just that I have things to take care of back at the office. I only took off two days. I know I should have told you. I thought we'd be going back tonight. If I don't show up for work in the morning, people at the foundation are going to wonder where I am." Joselyn figured if he could lie, so could she. But he did it better, and they both knew it. She wanted desperately to get ahold of Paul. Tell him where she was and have him call the base so the MPs would come and get her.

"Why don't you call your office? Tell them you're gonna be another day or two," said Akers.

"I thought about it, but my phone's not working. There's no signal."

"Really?" Akers pulled his cell phone out of his pocket and looked at it. "You know, you're right. I'm not getting anything either. That's strange. The last time I was here, I had no problem at all. Maybe they're working on the towers. Why don't you just go ahead and use the land-line?" He gestured toward the phone on the table.

"Maybe I will," she said. "Later." She sensed that any signal for help would set him off. "I was thinking maybe we could go over to the mission, so I could take my camera and get some pictures. You said earlier . . ."

"No. That's not possible," he said. "Henley might see us driving around." As he spoke, he was busy in the kitchen, pouring a bottle of sparkling water into two glasses. He turned and handed a glass to her. "Here; the water in this place tastes like crap," said Akers.

The astringent soda water tasted good. It quenched her thirst.

"Maybe you're right," she said. "But I don't really want to sit around here all day with nothing to do. Maybe we could take the car and head off base. If we're not here, he can't see us."

"Where do you want go?"

"I don't know." She certainly didn't want to go with him for a ride in the country. She was looking for any-place where there were people, where she might lose her-self in a crowd or find help. "I know," she said. "Maybe we could go to San Simeon. See the castle. I've never been there. And it can't be that far."

"You know, you're starting to sound like my wife."

"How's that?" she said.

"Anything to get away from me."

"No, that's not what I was thinking at all."

"You look tired," he said. "I think maybe you should go lie down. Take a nap."

"I don't . . ."

"Do it anyway!" The way he said it, the tone in his voice and the look in his eye, made it clear this wasn't a suggestion.

"Maybe you're right." Joselyn turned and picked up her overnight bag, which was still on the floor in the outer room. She thought for a moment, and said: "Do you mind if I check out the rooms?"

"Help yourself."

She was trying to maintain civility, to keep it on a human plane, and if necessary, even to keep him interested. Anything to get away. Instinct told her that once things ruptured irredeemably, there was no telling what he might do.

She headed for one of the bedrooms. She stepped inside, looked around, saw what she wanted, then sat on the bed as if she were testing the mattress.

Akers glanced at her a couple of times through the open door, a sullen expression on his face.

She leaned toward the head of the bed and looked behind the door to see if there was a lock on the inside. There wasn't.

She crossed the living room and did a tour of the bedroom on the other side. It was the same. Both rooms had the same amenities. Neither one of them had a door that locked. But both of them had extension telephones on the bedside tables. Joselyn leaned through the open door of the second room, smiled broadly at Akers, and said: "I think I'll take this one if you don't mind."

"Whatever."

"Do you have a preference?" she asked.

"Would it matter?"

"Of course it would. If you prefer this room I'll take the other, it's fine."

"You decide," he said. "You seem to know everything else."

The last thing she wanted to do was argue with him. His mood was impossible to gauge. One minute he was euphoric, hopelessly in love, the next he was petulant, irritable, and sulking.

"Later, I'll cook dinner if you like."

"We'll see," he said.

She stepped back inside and closed the bedroom door behind her.

She walked straight to the ladder-back chair against the wall. It was solid oak and heavy. Joselyn carried it to the door, and, trying not to make a sound, she propped the back of the chair under the brass doorknob.

She stepped to the side of the bed and started to reach for the phone. Then she stopped and thought for a moment. Given his level of paranoia, Akers might be testing her, listening in on the phone in the other room.

Slowly, as if she was defusing a bomb, Joselyn carefully lifted the receiver, replacing its weight with her finger on the button in the center of the cradle. She held the button down, raised the receiver to her ear, then slowly lifted her finger as she listened. She strained to hear any sound of Akers breathing on the line. Instead, there was stone-dead silence, nothing, no sound at all.

She reached down and pressed zero on the phone. The

line was dead. She dropped the receiver on the bed and lifted the phone from the table. There, underneath it, lay the severed end of the telephone line. The tiny plastic jack in the back of the phone was missing.

Akers had cut the line and removed the jack so there was no way to fix it. Then she remembered. When they first arrived in the room he had tested both of the beds. When he finally came out, he was cleaning his nails with one of those small, folding, tactical knives, the kind with razor-sharp blades and a box cutter.

Suddenly, she was exhausted. She couldn't keep her eyes open. The stress, the tension was catching up with her. Maybe if she relaxed, lay down for just a few minutes, she could think more clearly. She settled onto the bed and put her head down on the pillow. The next thing she knew she was out.

AKERS FOLDED THE knife and put it back in his pocket. He didn't bother to hide the severed wire from the phone in the living room. Instead, he just let it fall to the floor. He knew that by now she would have discovered the one in the bedroom.

He reached into his other pocket and pulled out a small, black plastic box. It was about the size of a pack of cigarettes. It was a pocket-sized portable electronic jammer. Used to jam radio signals across a broadband, it would block cell phone, Wi-Fi, and Bluetooth signals for anything within a hundred meters. The military used them on missions where it was critical to shut down local cell communication in case the air cover failed to take out fixed infrastructure.

He checked to make sure the jammer was on and the batteries fresh. Then he dropped it into the center drawer of a table in the living room and closed the drawer. From there, it would block any cell signal in the suite, just in case she tried to use her phone again.

Chapter 17

HARRY WONDERED IF they had cleared the mountains and, if so, whether he could reach Herman on his cell phone. But as he thought about it, he figured, why bother? There was nothing they could do from way up there.

The call for Paul from the woman named Boggs was probably nothing. At least Harry hoped that was the case.

Boggs sounded like a busybody pain in the ass. When she told him about the dog, Harry told her to call the pound. She yelled at him over the phone and accused him of being insensitive. To Harry, insensitivity was part of his DNA. It was like calling Aristotle a Greek.

She told him about the pooch and the dirty laundry, the fact that Akers had a dangerous job, that his life had been threatened, and that the family, the wife and two kids, hadn't been seen in three days now. She told him that she knew Allyson Akers as well as she knew her own daughter, and that to go off like that without so much as a phone call was not like her. Intuition told her that something was wrong.

No single item on her list of worries and clues made a dent on Harry. He was about to tell her to take two aspirin for her intuition and call him in the morning. He might have hung up on her except for one thing—what Boggs told him about the dog.

She explained that she had fed and watered the animal. The poor creature looked as if it hadn't eaten in days. What she told him next was what caught Harry's attention. After Gypsy finished eating, it wandered around the kitchen aimlessly for some time. Periodically, it scratched at the back door. Every once in a while, it would go to the front door and do the same thing there.

Boggs told Harry that she had taken care of the dog on several occasions before when Allyson and the kids were away, and that Gypsy had never acted like this.

Given the food the dog had consumed, Boggs figured the animal needed to relieve itself. So she opened the back door, following it out into her yard to keep an eye on it. She told Harry that's when it happened.

The dog darted through a small hole at the corner of her fence, and from there across Allyson Akers's backyard. In the flash of an eye, it dove through the doggie door at the back of Akers's house and disappeared inside.

Boggs hadn't seen the animal since. No matter what she did, she was unable to entice the dog back to the door. Gypsy was inside the house somewhere, but Boggs couldn't see her.

Harry might have dismissed it and told her that when

the dog gets hungry, it'll come back. But he didn't because he had seen this before.

BY THE TIME Harry pulled up in front of the house, Joanna Boggs was already standing on her front lawn, wringing her hands and waiting for him.

"I thought you'd never get here."

"Came as fast as I could," said Harry. "Any sign of the dog?"

She shook her head.

"Is it making any noise? Barking?"

"No. Not that I can hear."

"Let's take a look," said Harry.

Boggs led the way. They went up the driveway along the side of the garage, through the gate and into the yard. She showed him the doggie door.

"Do you want me to call her again?" she asked. "I mean I don't mind calling her."

"Even if she comes, I doubt she's gonna be able to tell us much," said Harry. "It's not the dog I'm worried about."

"Oh God!" Boggs backed up a couple of steps and put the fingers of both hands to her mouth. "Maybe I made a mistake. Maybe I shouldn't have called you."

"Too late now," said Harry.

"What can I do?"

"Can you get me a kitchen knife?"

"Do you want something really sharp?"

"Normal tableware will do," he told her.

A couple of minutes later, she was back with a single

stainless-steel knife. The edge on the blade was as dull as a spoon.

"Anything else?"

"No. Just stay here. Keep an eye in case they happen to come back, or somebody else comes to the house. Tell them who I am. And please not to shoot me." Harry took off his jacket and tie and handed them to her. "Here, you can hang on to these."

"Sure."

He undid the top button on his shirt, climbed the couple of steps to the back door, and looked through the glass panel on the top. It would have been easy to break it, reach inside, and open the door, but Harry figured it might be better if he only committed half of the crime of "breaking and entering."

He pressed his face to the glass, looking to see if there was a safety chain. There wasn't. Thank God for little favors, he told himself.

He got down on one knee. He pushed the flap of the dog door through to the inside, then looked through the opening. He could see past the service porch and into the kitchen. He saw nothing unusual.

He wished the dog had been bigger, in which case the opening would have been larger. But it wasn't.

Harry took the knife, put the tip of the blade on the concrete landing outside the door and pushed on it until the thin steel bent. He kept working on it until he turned the blade into a rough approximation of the letter L. He put his hand with the knife through the opening in the doggie door until the upturned blade hooked the back of the grey neoprene flap. Then he pulled the knife back through the opening. The flap followed. He lifted it up on the outside of the door so that it was out of the way.

Harry turned over on his back and stuck his head through the opening. He could see the doorknob with its lock a little more than two feet above the tip of his nose. If his tongue had been longer, he could have wrapped it around the doorknob and opened and turned it. As it was, he was going to have to get one arm along with his head through the rectangular opening. Harry remembered a trip to Thailand and seeing monkeys who had been trained to climbed trees and knock down coconuts. About now he was wishing he could rent one.

He slid his head to the right and brought his left hand up into the opening. The problem was the bend in the elbow. He might be able to work it through so that his arm, up to the shoulder, was inside.

After a couple of minutes, some effort, and not a little sweat, Harry got his arm inside. How he was going to get it out was another question. He reached up and turned the knob. Pressed by the upper part of Harry's body, the door popped open.

"Oh! Oh! You got it," said Boggs.

"Ma'am, it's a matter of debate who's got what," said Harry. "Maybe you can give me a hand, come over, and pull me out of here."

A couple of minutes later, Harry was back on his feet, a small rip in his dress shirt under his left arm. Otherwise, no worse for the wear. "Now that's the easy part," said Harry. "Let's hope we don't find anything inside. You stay here."

Harry went in. It took him less than a minute to clear the downstairs. Other than some dust and a few children's toys scattered across the carpet in the living room, there was no evidence of any crime except the one Harry had committed in coming through the back door.

He went upstairs. There was a short hallway with what looked like three bedrooms. The doors were closed on two of them. He assumed, based on the various knickknacks, hand-printed signs, and glow-in-the-dark objects pinned and glued on the outside that these two closed doors led to the children's rooms. Harry couldn't see anything, but his nose was already telling him there was something wrong.

Harry took out a handkerchief from his pocket and used it to turn the knob on the first door. It swung open. Inside was a sea of chaos, stuffed animals and toys tossed everywhere. There was a storm of rumpled blankets and pillows on top of the bed.

Harry stepped inside to take a closer look. He used his handkerchiefed hand to turn on the light, then reached over and grabbed a pony on a stick from a barrel of toys. He used the pole from the pony's body to poke through the blankets and pillows on the bed. There was nothing there. No sign of a child. He looked in the closet. It was a confusion of clothes and sundry items, but nothing bad.

He moved on to the next room. It was much the same though a little neater. Harry assumed that this might belong to the older of the two boys. There were pictures on the wall and a few toy guns. A small computer sat on a table in the corner. One of the photographs pinned to the wall was a shot of Cam Akers with some other men, all dressed in camo gear holding assault rifles. The stark, barren mountains in the distant background offered a hint of Afghanistan, or maybe the tribal regions of Pakistan. In the photograph, Akers's face, the skin peeling and parched, looked much thinner than Harry remembered it. His cheeks were drawn and hollow. From the picture, it was clear that Akers had paid a heavy price for his service.

He stepped out of the room, closed the door, and moved down the hall toward the sunlit room at the end. Here the door was open. With each step, the dense odor of putrefaction become stronger. Before he reached the door, it overwhelmed him. He put the handkerchief to his mouth and nose and kept walking as he held the pole pony in the other hand. Here Harry touched nothing. This was a crime scene, and he knew it.

At the open door, he finally saw her. A woman perhaps in her late twenties, though it was difficult to tell from rigor that has drawn her lips back into a tight, rigid smile of death. This mirrored the larger macabre crescent beneath her chin, where the blade wielded by her killer had opened her throat. She lay sprawled on the bed, dressed in a cream-colored nightgown that might once have been white. Harry couldn't tell.

Her eyes were open to the sky. Drained of the rose color of life, her flesh was white as new-fallen snow, though in places splotches in various other shades running to black had already begun to turn. The brown hue of putrefied blood had congealed in the folds of the bedcovers like rivers of rust. It pooled in a low reservoir formed by the mass of body weight in a moat surrounding her hips.

Her right arm hung off the edge of the bed angled toward the floor. Her dead, limp fingers dangled above the small dog huddled on the floor beneath them, as if waiting to be caressed by its mistress one last time. The fact that the bed was so high and the dog so small prevented her from making the leap that would have no doubt transformed the pooch into a bloody paintbrush, the four-legged messenger of death.

Harry looked around, his eyes carefully scanning the corners of the room and the dark recesses of the open closet, looking for the two children. He checked the connecting bath and took a quick look under the bed, but there was no sign of them.

He used the pole from the pony to prod the dog away from the bed, then scooped it up in one hand and headed back down the hall toward the stairs. He opened the door, pitched the pony pole back into the child's room, then reached into his pocket for his cell phone. Harry punched in 9-1-1, and a few seconds later said: "I want to report a homicide. . . ."

Chapter 18

By the time Joselyn finally woke up, it was dark outside. She seemed dazed, confused. She must have been exhausted, she thought. She had slept for hours. It seemed like a bad dream. But now that she was awake, locked away in the bedroom in a strange building knowing he was outside her door, and she could hear him moving around in the kitchen, it was becoming a nightmare. It took her a several minutes to gather herself, to work up enough nerve to come out of the bedroom and face him again.

Akers was pouring milk over cereal in a bowl at the kitchen counter.

"I thought you wanted me to cook."

"Tonight, this'll do." He said it with his back to her in a near mumble.

"Fine." So much for steaks and champagne. Not that Joselyn cared. She had long since lost her appetite, her mind occupied with other more pressing matters, whether Akers was truly dangerous. She didn't want to press the matter to find out. What she wanted was a way out. His mood hadn't changed. If anything, he seemed even more morose. He was no longer the man of adventure, firing rapid rounds of wit. Now every reply was rationed, limited to as few words as possible.

Joselyn lifted the lid and looked at the groceries in the ice chest. Most of the ice had turned to water. Nothing had been put in the refrigerator. Perhaps he was waiting for her to do it. Woman's work.

She spied a square of cheese, Asiago, shrink sealed in heavy plastic, floating in the bottom. She rescued it, grabbed an apple and a small container of yogurt, and retreated to the kitchen to find a spoon for the yogurt and a knife to cut the cheese.

"I'll cut that for you," he told her.

"I can do it."

"No, you can't."

When she opened the drawer, she found out why. All of the knives were gone. Forks as well. There was nothing in the drawer sharper than a teaspoon. If she wanted to get the plastic wrap off the cheese, she would have to gnaw it with her teeth.

"Where's all the silverware?"

"Guess they lost it," he told her. "You know how it is. Souvenir hunters."

"Yeah, I'd want that stuff for my collection. Wonder if it was the same people who chewed through the phone lines."

He shot her a look that made her think maybe it wasn't wise to run her mouth and get lippy with him. Nurture his fantasies, and maybe she might make it through the night.

"Here, give me that." He reached out.

She handed him the cheese.

Akers pulled the folding tactical knife from his pocket, flicked open the blade, and sliced through the plastic like it was melted butter. He peeled it back and cut several pieces of the dry, hard cheese. He slipped one of the slices, resting on the flat surface of the blade, into his mouth.

She watched as it disappeared.

He sliced another, left it on the knife, reached over and fed it to her.

"It's good, isn't it?"

"Yeah, but it should be sliced very thin," said Joselyn. "Can I do it?"

"Not with my knife. I'm afraid you might cut yourself. Then how would I feel?" He sliced a few more pieces, then closed the blade and put the knife back in his pocket.

Joselyn ate the cheese and the apple between spoonfuls of yogurt. She was hungrier than she thought. When she finished, she put the rest of the cheese in the ice, tossed the empty yogurt container in the trash, and said: "Do you mind if I take a shower?"

"Not if I can watch," he said.

When she turned to look at him, it was like someone had flipped a switch. The jock was back. Big grin on his face. Suddenly, he wanted to party. It caught her off balance. She thought for a second and realized maybe it was an opportunity. If she threw cold water on him, Mr. Hyde might come back.

"Do you like to watch?" she asked.

"I don't know. I've never done it. I was just giving you a bad time."

"You like to do that, don't you? Give me a bad time."

"It's fun. Most of the time, I'm kidding around. Go ahead and take a shower. I won't bother you."

"Can I trust you?"

"I don't know. Let's find out. Could be fun," he said.

She looked at the clock over the stove. It was almost 9:00 P.M. Joselyn had slept away the entire afternoon and early evening. She wondered if he had drugged her, the soda water he'd given her earlier in the day. Akers had pulled all the curtains closed across the windows of the living room and shut down the blinds in the small kitchen window. It was like he was hiding in a cave.

"Aren't you tired?" she asked.

"Little bit, I suppose," he said.

"Maybe if we get a good night's sleep, we'll wake up refreshed in the morning," said Joselyn.

"Yeah, but I have a hard time sleeping," he told her.

"Maybe you should take something for that."

"No. I like to sleep light. Besides, I don't like taking stuff that messes with my head."

"That's wise."

It gave Joselyn an idea. "How about a cup of tea?" she said. "I've got some in my bag in the other room. It's something new. I've never tried it before. But it might be fun tonight."

"What is it?"

"A friend recommended it. She says I'm frigid. I think she's crazy. It's supposed to be an aphrodisiac."

"Really?"

"I bought it in San Francisco a few weeks ago. It's probably nothing but a scam. They say it comes from China."

"That would make sense," said Akers. "How else are you gonna get a billion and a half people?"

"The guy who sold it to me says it turns women into nymphomaniacs and makes men hard as a rock. Of course, the guy's a salesman, and he's selling the stuff. So take it with a grain of salt. Stands to reason, anything that powerful would require a prescription, don't you think?"

"Maybe we should find out," said Akers.

"I'm game if you are. Let me change and get ready to shower. I'll make the tea. We'll have some. Then I'll take my shower, and we'll see what happens."

"I'm thinking that to make you horny, it's gonna have to be a fucking wonder drug," said Akers. "Two days, and I haven't been able to get near you."

"Like I say, I wouldn't expect too much," said Joselyn. "But you never know. Let me go get ready."

"Yeah, go ahead. Put on something comfortable," he said.

She headed for the bedroom, went inside, and closed the door. Joselyn grabbed her purse and found the small plastic tube with the cap on it inside. If he had drugged her earlier in the day, she was about to return the favor. Her prescription was for Ambien, sleep medication, a full thirty-day supply. She took out three tablets, started to put the top back on the bottle, thought about it, and took out one more. She knew she would lose some of it in the process of crushing the pills and probably a little more getting it into the tea. She didn't want to kill him, but she wanted to put him down long enough to get away.

She looked around the room for something she could use to crush the tablets. The best she could come up with was the hard metal edge of a compact from her purse. She used a piece of plate glass covering the top of the bureau, put the pills on it one at a time, and used the compact to turn them to powder. It took several minutes. She was working on the last pill when he knocked on the door, and asked: "What's taking so long?"

"You have to be patient. Give a girl some time and a little privacy," she said.

"I'll wait, but hurry it up."

She listened as he walked away from the door. Joselyn reached into her purse and pulled out a packet of chewing gum. She slid out one stick, unwrapped the metal foil from around it, and tossed the gum in the waste can. Then she flattened out the metal foil on the glass top of the bureau and used her finger to sweep the sleeping powder onto the foil. When she had gathered as much of it as she could onto the foil, she folded it up into a tight little packet and tossed it on the bed.

Then she scrambled to get into something that might keep him distracted until she could visit him with the sandman. Unfortunately, Joselyn hadn't come prepared to seduce him. There were no lacy underthings in her overnight bag, lingerie from Victoria's Secret or baby dolls from Frederick's. She best she could do were a pair of sheer bikini panties with a small heart printed in a strategic location and a loose-fitting nightshirt that hung off one shoulder, which, if she maneuvered it skillfully, might keep him on the edge long enough to put him to sleep. Joselyn knew that it wasn't the packaging that mattered but what was in the box. The trick was to keep all the parts moving fast enough so that he couldn't get his hands on it long enough to open it.

Then she remembered. She'd purchased a pair of thigh-high nylons for a costume party at Halloween. She never wore them because she never made it to the party. But she had slipped them into one of the outer pockets of her traveling bag. She checked and, sure enough, the cellophane envelope with the smoke-colored nylons was inside. She slipped it out and ripped open the package.

"What the hell's taking so long in there?" He was outside the bedroom door knocking.

"Wait and see. You're gonna like it," she told him.

She pointed her toes and slipped on one of the nylons, pulled it up her leg, and allowed the tight elastic to close around her thigh. Then she worked in the mirror to straighten the seam in the back. She repeated the process with the other leg. The effect wasn't quite the same without heels. But it was better than baggy sweats and running shoes.

When she looked in the mirror and worked the nightshirt to effect, the nylons offered a tantalizing glimpse of the "no go zone," the area above the dark elastic of the thigh-highs and the lower edge of the bikini panties. The only question was whether she could dodge his hands long enough for the Ambien to sneak up and whack him.

She walked over to the bed and picked up the small foil packet with the powder. The problem was where to hide it. She opted for the elastic band on the nylons at the inside of her right thigh. She slipped the packet under the tight synthetic material and felt with her fingers along the outside of the stocking until she was satisfied that the foil wouldn't slide down her leg.

She grabbed two tea bags from the traveling pack in her bag. It was some kind of spice tea from Ceylon. She also plucked two packets of Equal, then reached in and got one more. She wanted to make sure she had something sufficiently sweet to cover the bitter taste of the Ambien.

She checked herself in the mirror one last time, took a deep breath, and headed for the door.

Chapter 19

HARRY STOOD INSIDE the yellow tape that now bordered Allyson Akers's house in Chula Vista. The street out in front was a mass of humanity, patrol cars, neighbors, several satellite vans from the media, and reporters all hawking for the story. In front of the driveway, at the curb, was the coroner's meat wagon. Forensics had been working the scene for almost four hours.

It was dark and Harry was tired. Sitting in a chair on her front porch, Joanna Boggs had a drawn, vacant expression, as if she had gone catatonic. She wanted to know where the children were and whether they were safe. It was the same question on the lips of everyone now that the media had picked up the story that the two kids were missing.

"Take it you're Mr. Hinds?"

When Harry turned, he saw a man in uniform standing behind him. But he wasn't with the police.

"I'm Captain Norman Shivers," he said. "I'm a medical doctor attached to North Island Naval. I understand you found the body?"

"That's correct," said Harry.

"The police also told me that you met with Mr. Akers professionally."

"Not exactly," said Harry. He explained the situation: that Herman had brought Akers to the office and that Harry's partner was the one who actually talked to him, but that they had determined not to take the case because, in their view, there wasn't one, at least not at that time.

"I was treating Chief Akers at the time that he left the military. We were in the process of trying to move his file and treatment over to the V.A., but," he said, "I'm afraid we weren't very successful."

Harry knew better than to ask him pointed questions concerning Akers's medical condition. Instead, he said: "What's your specialty?"

"Psychiatry," said Shivers.

"PTSD," said Harry, posttraumatic stress disorder. Looking back at Akers, his conduct that night at the restaurant, it was starting to make sense.

"Did he talk to you or your partner about his experiences?" asked the doctor.

"We didn't take his case," said Harry, "but the contents of his consultation are privileged."

"I understand," said Shivers, "but we now have a man on the run who we know is very unstable and dangerous. We have two minor children who are missing, and if you know anything that might help us find them . . ."

"I get it," said Harry. "To my knowledge, he never said

anything that could provide a clue as to where the children might be. The cause of his concern, at least what was stated, without violating any serious confidences, was his fear that the federal government was gearing up to bring a case against him."

"Because of leaks concerning classified information relating to high-level missions," said Shivers. "And the fact that he was discharged because of this."

"Then you already know."

"He was discharged because of psychiatric disorders. I am going to confide in you because we have an ongoing situation here," said Shivers. "And whether you know it or not, you may know something that might help us find him."

Harry listened.

"Do you know where he is?"

"Not with any certainty," said Harry.

"So you're telling me you have a hunch?"

Harry gave him an equivocal expression.

"We've been working with local authorities while at the same time trying to keep it under wraps," said Shivers, "because Akers is high-profile in terms of his background."

"So he wasn't lying about Abbottabad?" said Harry.

Shivers shook his head. "The restraining order was issued because of threats he had made to his wife and family. Akers was furious. We know that. It may be the reason he killed her."

"Of course, that assumes that he did it," said Harry. He didn't carry any torch for Akers, but there was no solid evidence as yet.

"The Navy wanted her to commit him for treatment, an institution," said Shivers.

"You mean for the criminally insane?"

"No, because he hadn't committed any crime of which we were aware, up to that point," said Shivers. "She refused to commit him. We urged her to do it. We didn't have any authority. She was afraid of him, but she still loved him. It was an impossible situation. The man had tried to kill himself twice, and he had been taking some severe risks on missions before he was discharged. It was as if he had a death wish, and it was endangering other people. We had no choice but to remove him from DEVGRU and ultimately discharge him."

"He told us that *he* made the decision to leave the military."

"He did," said Shivers, "because we told him that if he stayed, he would be required to undergo treatment. It's a terrible thing," said the doctor, "the trauma of long-term combat. The human psyche is not designed to cope with the ceaseless terror of violent, daily death. The deafening sounds, the smell, the concussive forces, the sudden loss of people you've come to think of as near siblings. Actually, that's wrong. They're often closer than siblings. Add to that the horrific things they're forced to witness and at times engage in. To tell you the truth, as bad as it is, and it is bad, I'm surprised that the traumatic effects are not worse. Add to that the nature of the volunteer force, the limited manpower in these wars, and their duration— many of these people are trying to cope with multiple long-term deployments and no real relief. And the politicians are wondering why the V.A. isn't functioning properly. They don't want to go back to the draft because that's not politically convenient."

Suddenly, there was a commotion from beyond the yellow tape out in the street. Reporters surrounded one of the detectives, a guy in plain clothes, and began pummeling him with questions. "There's a rumor you've found the children. Are they alive?" The detective ignored them, brushed past the bristling microphones, under the tape, and approached Shivers. He cupped one hand and whispered in the doctor's ear.

"It's OK," said Shivers. "You can talk in front of him. I believe Mr. Hinds wants to help us."

"They found the kids," said the detective. "They're both alive."

"Where were they?" asked Shivers.

"With their aunt. Akers's sister up in L.A. She says he dropped them off," the cop looks at his notebook, "early morning on the third, about 2:00 A.M."

Harry thought for a moment. He tried to recall whether that was the morning after their drinks at the Brigantine.

"Apparently, according to what the oldest boy told child services, Akers must have come over here, slipped into the house late at night, killed the wife, and told the children that mama was sleeping," said the detective. "He put the kids in the car and drove north. He told his sister there was a family emergency, and before she could ask any questions, he was gone. We're still trying to get a lead on where he is."

Until that very moment, there had been no hard evidence that Akers was the killer. Perhaps a preponderance of suspicion but nothing more. Assuming the information from the child was accurate, that had now changed. If Paul and Herman were right, and Joselyn was with Akers, she was in serious danger, and his friends were headed toward possible disaster. A confrontation with a man like Akers, who was conditioned to kill on an almost daily basis, could leave one or all of them dead.

"Do you know where he is?" Shivers looked at Harry.

"I need to make a phone call," he told him.

"By all means," said the doctor. He told the cop to give Harry a little space, and they both stepped away. The detective continued to study him from under hooded eyes. He saw Harry as the criminal defender, enemy at the gates.

Harry reached for his cell phone and punched the quick-dial button for Paul's cell number. He had already called earlier and told them of the gory discovery, Allyson Akers's body. Paul had cut to the core and asked the pivotal question, whether the coroner or anyone else could fix with certainty the date and time of death. The issue was whether Akers was even in town at the time. It could be that he and Joselyn had already left. In which case, Joselyn would be his ironclad alibi. Now that was gone. The events had seemingly fixed the time of the murder. If Allyson was alive when Akers took the kids, she would have called the police. He was violating the restraining order. She didn't because she couldn't. She was dead. Akers had killed her. What had once appeared to Harry as a long shot, the specter of Joselyn and Akers camped on a military post in a remote area of Central California, was beginning to take on the specter of a nightmare.

Chapter 20

THE SECOND JOSELYN opened the bedroom door, Akers turned, looked at her, and said: "Wow! You do polish up nice, don't you?" He stood in the living room, looking over the back of the couch, taking her in with hungry eyes.

When he started to walk toward her, she said: "No, you stay right there and let me make the tea. Then we'll cozy up on the couch and talk."

"Whatever you say."

Joselyn turned and walked to the kitchen. There was an electric kettle for boiling water. She filled it, made sure it was plugged in, hit the button, and turned it on. She grabbed two cups, mugs from the cupboard over the sink. She saw a large four-cup French press for making coffee and took that down, too. She took the mechanical press out of its clear glass carafe. This she would use to steep the tea, then pour two cups, one of which she would lace with the Ambien for Akers. There was no chance of confusion since the mugs bore different colors, one red, one blue.

"So you think this stuff will work?" He was talking about the aphrodisiac that was supposed to be in the tea.

"Oh, yeah!" She was talking about the Ambien that would be there instead. She listened as the electric kettle began to boil the water. She dropped both tea bags into the glass carafe from the press and stood there tapping her fingernails on the countertop.

"Can I help you?"

"No, no. This is my job," she said. "Why don't you take a load off? Sit down on the couch. I'll be there in a minute." That way his back would be to the open kitchen. He'd be less likely to see what she was doing.

"I'm tired of sitting," he said. "Besides, I like watching you. That is a sexy outfit. We're gonna have to go shopping sometime."

"That would be nice." She was fine with it just as long as the place was crowded with plenty of armed security. She turned to look at him. He was standing there staring at her. She smiled, comely but nervous. How she was going to get the foil packet out of the top of her nylons with him watching was a mystery The second he saw her hand move to her upper thigh, he would want to come over and help. "Can you do me a favor?"

"What do you need?"

"Can you check the bathroom? I couldn't find my dark glasses earlier. I think I might have left them in there."

"Sure."

She heard the rubber soles of his light tactical boots squeak on the hardwood floor as he turned and walked toward the bathroom. Immediately she reached down, fished for the foil packet, took it out, and unfolded it. She started to pour the powder into the red mug.

"I don't see 'em."

"They've gotta be there. I can't find 'em anywhere else. Keep looking."

"You sure?"

"Yeah." Her hands were shaking. She only intended to pour part of the contents into the cup. She couldn't be sure how potent it might be. Finally, she poured it all, quickly balled up the used foil, and tossed it into the open wastebasket. She immediately ripped open two of the packets of Equal and poured them in on top, then tossed the little blue packs in the trash as well. The water reached a boil and the electric kettle shut down. She filled the carafe with hot water. The tea began to steep.

An instant later, he came out of the bathroom. "They're not in there."

"I musta left 'em in the car," she said.

"We can check in the morning," said Akers. Instead of going back to the couch, he wandered into the kitchen, moved up close behind her, and put his hands around her waist.

Joselyn could feel his hot breath on her naked shoulder. She wanted to put her hand over the open mug to cover the white powder in the bottom, but she didn't dare. It might fire his paranoia the minute he saw her make the move. She was hoping he wouldn't look down.

Then he leaned forward, kissed her on the nape of the neck, and said: "What's that?"

"What?"

"That stuff in the cup."

"Oh, that. Some Equal," she said. "You do use sweetener?"

"The only sweet thing I need right now is you. Coffee and tea, I take *au naturel*. And you and I can try some of the same later."

"Fine, I'll toss it. I'm not partial to sweeteners either."

"I'll take the blue cup," he said.

"Whatever you like. Now let me finish up here," she said. "You go back out there and wait." She tried to sound motherly, hoping he would take directions. He did.

The second he stepped back, turned, and walked away, she dumped the contents of the red mug into the blue one. She thought for a moment, then took the last packet of Equal and poured it into to the red mug, the one she would be drinking from.

Minutes later, they were seated on the couch, the two mugs in front of them on the low coffee table. Akers had his hands all over her, stroking the nylon on her upper thigh with his other hand around her shoulder. He kissed her on the lips.

"If you're like this now, what are you gonna be like after the tea?" she asked.

"I don't know."

"Why don't we find out," she said.

"Sure." He reached down, picked up the blue mug, and took a sip. She did the same with the red one.

"That's awful sweet," he said. "You sure I got the right cup?"

"I think it's the tea," said Joselyn. "Probably an herbal blend. Mine is sweet, too."

He reached over, took the mug from her hand, and tasted it. "You're right. The only problem is it's a little hot for me. Lemme put a little cold water in it."

"Here, let me get that for you."

"No. No you stay there," he said.

He got up and carried the cup to the kitchen. He stood in front of the sink with his broad back to her, so she couldn't see what he was doing. But she heard him turn on the water.

"You know, the tap water here tastes like shit," he said.

He left it running with the mug on the counter as he went to the ice chest and pulled out a bottle of water. Then he went back to the counter to cool off the tea. A few seconds later, he turned off the lights in the kitchen and came back to the couch. He gulped down the tea and sat there, leering at her. She had done it! Now if she could only endure the wrestling match that was to follow and give the drug time to work.

"Listen, I'm gonna take my shower."

"I like you the way you are."

"You'll like me a lot more once I wash off the sweat of the road."

"Go ahead, just don't take too long."

She did. She immediately went back to the bedroom, grabbed her street clothes and her running shoes, and wrapped them in one of the large guest bath towels, then headed for the bathroom. He glanced at her and smiled as she walked by, reached out over the back of the couch, and patted her on the ass. Fortunately, he didn't check the bath towel tucked like a football under her outside arm.

"Back in a minute," she said. She went into the bathroom and closed the door. She turned on the shower but she didn't get in. Instead, she changed her clothes, sat on the closed toilet lid, and waited. She wasn't sure how much time passed, but he wasn't hollering for her to hurry up. It was a good sign. Finally, she got up, went to the door, and opened it just a crack. The sound of the shower covered any noise. He was sprawled on the couch, his head lying back as if maybe he was asleep. Then he suddenly shook himself awake, offered up a massive yawn, struggled to his feet, and seemed to stumble toward the other bedroom.

She watched as he flipped off the lights in the living room, went into the bedroom, and closed the door. A few seconds later, the crack of light under the door went dark. He was down. She was sure of it. But to be certain, she waited, counted five hundred slowly.

She turned off the light in the bathroom but left the shower running, hoping it might cover any noise she made. When she opened the bathroom door, it was pitch-black in the living room, all the curtains drawn, the blinds shut. Joselyn was afraid she might trip over something. She was feeling with her hands, the only sure point of navigation, a sliver of light under the entry door leading to the stairs down from the tower. She moved toward it. Almost there, only a few feet to go. She could barely glimpse the outline of the door in the darkness ahead of her. Suddenly, she smelled something medicinal. It wafted on the air in the dark room.

She kept moving one foot in front of the other. The smell became stronger as she approached the door. It was coming from outside somewhere. It had to be. She felt the feathery wisp of threads at her throat. The back of her hand brushed the doorknob. She reached for it, and suddenly the stench covered her mouth, the foul odor filling her nostrils and streaming toward her stomach, almost making her retch. The cloth sealed her nose and mouth. Joselyn struggled, she fought, her knees buckled, head lulled back, her neck arched, and everything went black.

Akers dragged her limp body a few feet, reached over, and turned on a lamp in the corner. With the flare of green light, he ripped the night goggles from his head. He held the cloth tight to her face until he was sure she was out cold.

Akers knew that she had been playing games in the kitchen. He had tossed the cup of tea down the sink when the water was running and poured a fresh one from the leftovers in the glass pitcher. He figured that this was a common source and that she wouldn't be poisoning herself. After that, all that was required was a little acting.

Now he had work to do. He realized that the minute Henley had time, he would check with the Agency back at Langley and do a background on him. Sooner or later, they were going to find Allyson's body at the house in Chula Vista. Once the news hit the tube, it would go national. Navy SEAL, Team Six on the lam. If word of Henley's sighting of him here got to Langley, how long before they put the pieces together to track his trail?

He could have tied Joselyn up, but instead it was more efficient to allow the chloroform to do the job. He soaked the cloth one more time, turning his face away so that the fumes wouldn't get him. Then he positioned it over her mouth and nose and tied it off around her head with two large rubber bands. He tented the cloth up a bit so that she would draw air in with the ether. He was certain it would keep her out of commission for at least an hour, and that was all the time he needed. He left the small radio-jamming device in the drawer of the table in the living room just in case Joselyn stirred and made it to her cell phone before he could get back. Then he carried her to her bedroom and dumped her on the bed.

Chapter 21

HENLEY WAS PARKED in one of the spaces out in front of the Hacienda. It was just after 11:00 P.M. He was sitting in the small blue sedan with federal plates and signs on the doors that marked him as a government gofer. The car was a rolling piece of crap operated by the GSA.

But then Henley wasn't a field agent. He didn't rate a high-end rental car. He was considered a bean counter and got about as much respect as an auditor with the IRS. It was little wonder they raked every taxpayer over the coals. And Henley couldn't even do that. All he could do was try to blow the whistle on Defense Department contractors, all of whom had close, well-moneyed friends in Congress.

He was hoping to get off the base and back home to Virginia the next day. He had put enough heat on the people from Stanford and the contractor that he was confident they would be moving operations over to Moffitt at Sunnyvale soon.

He was talking on his cell phone with his driver's side window rolled down. It was unseasonably warm, but Henley was just minutes from his room and a cool shower. He was talking with one of his supervisors back at Langley, the boss on the night crew. They were wrapping up business, coming current on the dirt of the day, a lot of numbers with Henley genuflecting. He was hoping to leapfrog perhaps two GS ratings with his next promotion. A little browning of the nose never hurt.

"I guess that's about it." He was about to hang up when he said: "Oh, by the way, one more thing. There was a guy who dropped by here today, said he was with the SEALS, attached to DEVGRU. His name is Cameron Akers. I never met him before, but I've heard of him. Rumor is he claims to have made his bones at Abbottabad. Shot the man. Of course, we all know better." Henley liked to walk the talk. It made him feel as if he were part of the clan, ready to put on a tux and go screw Moneypenny at a moment's notice.

"The problem is, I don't know exactly what he was doing here. He didn't seem to have any real business. He showed up with some skirt on his arm. Probably trying to impress her. But here's the deal. Somewhere, I saw our man Akers musta taken a war wound or something."

As he was talking, a large, dark vehicle pulled into the parking space next to him on his left. With his window down and the guy's motor running, Henley could barely hear his boss at the other end of the line.

"What's the significance of all this?" said the boss.

The guy might have been a GS-15, but he was dense.

"Word is Akers was discharged for medical cause. If so, what's he doing here showing up on a classified project? You might want to check it out. Ordinarily, I wouldn't take a second look," said Henley, "but being as the Joint Chiefs and the Director are on the warpath trying to tighten security, I thought I better bring it to your attention. You know," said Henley, "before the FBI comes and tells you about it." He almost had to shout to be heard above the sound of the engine parked right next to him. Henley looked over at the other car, his expression filled with irritation. The entire parking lot was empty, and this asshole had to park on top of him. He was about to roll up his window when the engine from the car next to him shut down. He looked over but couldn't see the prick behind the wheel.

"You can't fix it if you don't know about it," said Henley. Protecting the boss was always the best way to a quick promotion. He would have asked that their telephone conversation be recorded and transcribed and that a copy be placed in his personnel file. But Henley figured since he was calling in through the Langley network, there were at least eighty people already listening in with digital-recording and transcription devices. By morning, his words would probably be all over WikiLeaks. It was the reason no one could keep secrets anymore.

"You might want to check it out and get back to me when you can. Talk to you tomorrow." Henley hung up.

The headlights went out on the car next to him. He looked over, but given the height of the vehicle and the fact that its windows were smoked, he couldn't see anyone inside. When he tried to open his door, he couldn't. The other car had him jammed in. "Damn it!"

He was forced to crawl across the front seat of the small sedan, open the passenger door and climb out headfirst. When he got there, Henley's eyes were focused down at the pavement less than two feet away. He looked a bit mystified. He wondered who the hell had spread the plastic poncho on the ground directly underneath the open car door, and more to the point, why?

Chapter 22

JOSELYN CAME TO in the dark bedroom. She was sprawled on her back across the bed. Her head throbbed. She ripped the cloth away from her face, snapping one of the rubber bands as she went. The cloth was dry. The ether had evaporated. She was nauseous, about to give up the tea and perhaps little pieces of apple from her earlier snack. Akers had drugged her with chloroform, and now it was making her sick. The question was where was he? The question was in the back of her mind as she retched.

She planted her hands on the bed and tried to stop the room from spinning. When it finally did, she took a deep breath and struggled to sit. Slowly, she dragged her legs over the side of the bed until they hit the floor. To Joselyn they sounded like two ten-pound flatirons.

She sat there for several seconds before she tried to stand. Joselyn knew that any second, Akers might charge into the room and douse her once more with the foul-smelling cloth. As she stood up, she stumbled forward, propelled by the forward cant of her upper body until she hit the wall several feet away. She thought that if Akers hadn't heard that, her head hitting the solid wall, he must be dead. Somehow, she knew he wasn't. She couldn't be that lucky. She was getting to know the man, and it was not a pleasant experience. She used the wall to hold herself up, both hands planted firmly against the flat surface. She looked out through the open bedroom door into the darkness beyond, the black void that was the living room.

Joselyn wondered how long she had been out and whether Akers was out there in the dark, waiting for her, toying with her like an alley cat with a mouse. That was his style.

Even if he was there, Joselyn knew she had no choice. She had to get down, out of the tower, or at least try. She stumbled out into the black void, dragging her listless legs and dead feet. Under the door in the distance, she could see the same sliver of bright light leading to the hallway outside, and beyond that, the stairs down to the lobby.

Joselyn made her way across the living room, lurching from one piece of furniture to the next until she ran into the back of the couch. She used it to steady herself and finally made it to the door.

She turned the handle, threw the door open, and instantly found herself bathed in the blinding light from the overhead fixtures out in the hall. She saw the top of the stairs just a short distance away. Best of all, there was no sign of Akers.

As she moved forward, the pulse in her head pounded.

Breath came in waves of near hyperventilation until she felt as if she might pass out. She had to keep going. She fought the fight, made it to the stairs, grabbed the railing, and started down.

When she finally got to the bottom, the ground level near the lobby, it seemed a miracle that she hadn't fallen. Her hopes crested and fell. The lobby was abandoned, the lights dimmed. There was no sign of the clerk at the desk. Perhaps they closed down for the night. Joselyn had no idea. Her eyes gravitated toward the couch against the wall. She wanted to sit, or better yet, lie down. But she knew if she did, she might never get up. The thought entered her mind that maybe the thing to do was to find someplace to hide, to huddle down where he couldn't find her, where she could sleep and recover her senses, then find help. But where?

She moved slowly toward the door, the entrance to the Hacienda. Joselyn knew she didn't want to step outside until she first looked to make sure that the Escalade wasn't parked there. Maybe he'd gone, taken the car, and disappeared? It was possible. With him, anything was possible. He was a nutcase. The thought of being abandoned by him certainly didn't fill her with a sense of loss. At the moment, the only picture she ever wanted to see of him in the future was on a wanted poster.

As she looked out through the front door, she saw only one car parked in front. It was a small sedan. The trunk was open. She could see the shadow of someone moving around near the rear of the vehicle just behind the open door to the trunk. It was the only living soul in sight.

Joselyn stepped out the door and started walking toward the car. As she drew closer she recognized it. She saw the federal government plate on the front, the light blue paint job. Then as she moved to the right she saw the sign on the driver's door FOR OFFICIAL USE ONLY. It was the car they'd seen at the airfield, the one Henley was driving, the only man Akers seemed to be afraid of. And there he was at the back of the car. Probably getting his luggage. Joselyn started to move faster. She picked up her feet and began to run. She reached the back of the car, turned, and smiled at the man standing there.

Before she realized what was happening, Akers put his hand over Joselyn's mouth to keep her from screaming. Her eyes took in the open trunk, the plastic, tarp-bound bundle inside. The bloody head of the man, Henley, under the flap of one corner.

Akers reached into the open trunk, doused another piece of cloth. Seconds later, the same familiar, sickening smell, the cloying odor of chloroform rose and swept over her one more time, carrying Joselyn away like a mountainous ocean wave.

Chapter 23

Akers tossed Joselyn into the backseat of the small sedan and slammed the door. He figured that he would do the final honors later. There was no need to tie her up. She was a rag doll, out cold for the second time, down for the count.

Ever since she took off her pretty clothes and tried to make for the door of the suite, Akers had been considering his options. At first he felt discouraged. He had wasted so much time and effort to make it work that, when she tried to poison him, naturally he was disappointed. He thought they really had a chance to make it. But she wasn't trying. She was an ice queen and high maintenance, way too much work.

So now he had two bodies to get rid of. The problem was transportation, how to move them and where to dump them? He would have preferred somewhere off base. There were millions of acres of open land and back roads in the area, places where no one would probably ever find them. The problem was, he had no way to deliver the goods.

He couldn't put the bodies in the back of the Escalade because there was no trunk. The back windows were smoked. It was difficult to see in, unless they stopped him at the guardhouse on his way out and checked. They might make him open up the back. This wasn't likely, but Akers couldn't be sure. And he didn't want to take the chance.

Henley's small blue sedan had a trunk, but Akers was sure to be challenged if he tried to drive it through the checkpoint and leave. The MPs were certain to have recorded the license plate and taken down Henley's information when he drove on post. They would have recorded his driver's license and perhaps his agency ID. Akers couldn't use either. If the guards took even a casual look at the picture on Henley's ID, there wasn't a hope in hell that Akers could pass for him.

The best he could do was to dump both bodies into the trunk of Henley's sedan, drive it to a secluded location somewhere on the base, and try to hide it. Put some brush over it or find a ravine where it couldn't be seen. He didn't want to burn it because they'd see the smoke for miles. With any luck, the military wouldn't find it for at least several days, maybe a week. By that time, he'd be long gone.

This was the plan for tonight's festivities. A ten- or fifteen-mile drive up one of the more secluded roads, with the headlights out, followed by a vigorous run back.

If he moved, he'd be back at the Hacienda by early morning. He could take a shower, grab the Escalade, load her up, and be gone before 10:00 A.M.

But before he could do anything, he had one more chore to complete. He had to gather up the wench's personal items, her clothes, the overnight bag, and anything else she left upstairs. He wanted to dump them along with the bodies in the trunk of the car.

Akers opened the back door, looked at her one more time, lifted one eyelid, and figured she was good for at least another forty minutes. By then, it wouldn't matter. She would be taking up residence in the trunk with Henley, getting ready to cook under the hot sun somewhere out in the wilds.

Akers closed the car door, locked it, and headed at a trot back to the room to grab her stuff.

Chapter 24

By THE TIME Herman and I rocket north on 101 past Camp Roberts, I've got the pedal to the metal doing eighty-five, not even bothering to check the rearview mirror any longer. If the Highway Patrol stops me now, I'm going to ask them to join us. We are told by authorities in San Diego that there's a nationwide BOLO (Be On The Look-out) for Cameron Akers, along with a description and warning that he is believed to be armed and dangerous.

Herman has made several attempts to call the Hacienda, but all he got was a recording and the message that the desk is closed for the night. Harry has a new friend, some shrink from the Navy who is preparing the ground for us with the military. As of fifteen minutes ago, Naval authorities from San Diego called ahead to Hunter Liggett so that the military police on base know what's happening.

An hour ago, we were told that they've checked their daily roster of visitors on base and that they showed no record of Akers having come on post. Then ten minutes ago they called back and said they had reason to believe that he might have entered the post under an alias, using a phony driver's license. One of their sergeants, an MP, remembered questioning a man near the airfield early this morning. He couldn't remember the name, but the man handed him a Navy SEAL ID showing that he was attached to DEVGRU. The description given fits Akers, that and the fact that there was a woman with him. I had Herman ask if there was a description for the woman. The sergeant said he didn't see her up close, but his partner who did, told him she was a "looker," a little bit older, but in his words, "a stone-cold fox."

BY THE TIME we reach the fort, there is a veritable task force forming a short distance down the road, inside the perimeter fence. I can see the emergency lights flashing from military vehicles in two or three directions. A few of the Humvees have mounted machine guns on the back. And most of the MPs appear to be packing carbines, mostly M-16s.

As we pull up to the gate, it appears that they're on the lookout for us. As soon as I roll down my window, a young lieutenant asks for my name. When I give it to him, he tells me to pull over and park the car in a reserved area. As Herman and I get out and lock up, another officer, this one in desert fatigues with captain's bars on his shoulders and packing heat on his side, crosses the road with an enlisted man, who is carrying two large boxes.

The officer approaches, and says: "Are you Mr. Madriani?"

"Yes."

"What can you tell us about the woman? Is she dangerous?"

"No! She doesn't have any idea what's going on. We believe she may have been lured up here believing he could help with some research. Items relating to her work."

"What kind of work?"

"Can we talk about that later? If she's with Akers, and she's who I think she is, she's in danger herself."

"How well do you know her?"

"Intimately," I tell him. "We live together."

"Oh," he says. "No one told us that. Do you know Akers?"

"Not well. I only met him once for a few hours, professionally and socially. He seemed somewhat erratic. But from everything I'm hearing now, he's dangerous as hell."

He nods. "She may be in trouble, but we can't be sure," he says.

"Who?"

"The woman. We've only had surveillance on them for about five minutes."

"Then you know where they are?"

"Yes. He's upstairs in a room at the Hacienda. She's in the backseat of a car parked in the lot out in front. She appears to be sitting upright, and every once in a while, she lies down. We don't know whether she's trying to conceal herself, whether she's armed, or whether she's under some kind of restraint that we can't see."

"If it's Joselyn, you should move in and get her out of there now."

"Given his background, there's a chance the car could be booby-trapped," he says.

"You mean a bomb?"

He nods. "In which case, she's a hostage."

"If I can get close enough to take a look, I can identify her. Then, at least, if it's her, you'll know who you're dealing with."

"Good!" he says. He grabs one of the boxes placed on the ground by the enlisted man. He lifts the lid and takes out a black Kevlar vest. "Here. Put this on!" He hands the other one to Herman. Seconds later, the officer, Herman, and I are packed into a Humvee with the driver and a guard, racing north up the road to a surveillance point where, I am told, I can get a look at the woman though a powerful spotting scope, clear enough that I should be able to identify her.

THE SECOND MAN 15

cold hand, what he does maybe or what but they in the some kind of each that we can't see.

"It's Joselyn, you should move in and get her out of there now.

"Given his background there's a chance the car could be booby-trapped.

...hardest the needs. "In which case, she's thoneat.

"If I can get close enough to take a look, I can identify her. She at least, if it's her, you you'll know who you're dealing with.

"Good," he says. He glances at the boxes placed on the ground by the enlisted man. He tilts the lid and takes

Chapter 25

AKERS SAW THEM coming a mile away. From the windows in the tower suite where he was gathering up Joselyn's clothes, nylons, and other goodies, he could see the emergency lights flickering all the way back to the main gate.

It didn't take a soothsayer to tell him what had happened. They had found Allyson's body down in Chula Vista, and now they had found him. He abandoned Joselyn's clothes and everything else, grabbed his pack from the other room, and flew out the door and down the stairs. In less than eight seconds, he was out the front door running toward the blue sedan parked in the lot.

If he had to make a run for it, he would have preferred to do it in the Escalade. It had much higher ground clearance and a lot more power. But parked where it was, down behind the tennis court, it was too far away. He considered ferrying, using one car to get to the other, but that would put him in the wrong direction, heading toward them. And they were closing on him fast.

He jumped into Henley's blue sedan and started the engine. Joselyn still lay in the backseat, drugged and half-conscious. She was moving around, trying to sit up, but from the look on her face, she had no idea where she was.

Akers backed up, then quickly swung around out of the lot. He looked to his right down Infantry Road and saw a line of flashing color—several vehicles coming up fast. Two more minutes, and they would have swarmed him inside the room.

He was hoping they knew that he had a woman on board. That way, at least, they wouldn't open up on him with the heavy artillery, a SAW gun or, worse, a MA Duce, a fifty-caliber Browning Machine mounted on top of one of the Humvees. It would turn the small sedan and everybody in it into filigreed lace.

As it was, he was going to have to drive like a son of a bitch to have any chance of getting away. As soon as he cleared the parking area, he took a sharp left.

He was trying to get around them to the south. If he could get outside the perimeter fence that surrounded the post, he might have a shot at getting to some of the open roads in the area. If he could lose himself in the hills, there was a slim chance he could slip away.

The minute he looked to his left, he knew it was hopeless. Everywhere was a sea of flashing lights. They were streaming up from the south. All of the roads in that direction were blocked.

He stopped for a moment to survey the terrain. They

were everywhere, like fire ants, flashing red dots as far as the eye could see. "Why? Why were they doing this? Why so many?" he wondered. "I'm only one man. Do they think I'm a god?" It was overkill. Akers knew it. At the same time, he realized, it was a tribute. Not to him personally but to his fighting skills. They were afraid of him. He had fought their wars and spilled his blood. Now he was home, and they were filled with fear. If only they knew. His arsenal of weapons was limited to the Ka-Bar, the small folding knife in his pocket, and his wits. Akers didn't have a firearm.

And he was rapidly running out of options. Ahead of him was a v-shaped intersection with three roads. Military vehicles with mounted machine guns blocked the two outer legs of the V. He could see them up the road, maybe a half mile out. The only route open was the one in the middle, a narrow thread of dusty sand that transected the V. It wasn't really a choice. Akers knew why they left it open. Like so many other things in his life, it was a dead end.

Chapter 26

I HAD NO problem identifying Joselyn in the back of the car. I told the captain, and he radioed instructions to have the vehicle surrounded and to seal off the building so as to trap Akers inside.

But it was too late. Before they could move, Akers came racing out the front door. He jumped in the car, backed out, and sped off, with Joselyn in the back.

"Tell your people not to shoot," I told the captain. We ran for the Humvee, and within seconds, we were in pursuit. We could see the small sedan ahead of us. There were two Humvees with military police between us and Akers's car. They came to an intersection and stopped. I didn't know why until we pulled up behind them. There in front of us, no more than thirty feet away, was Akers's vehicle, stopped in the middle of the road.

The gunner on the roof of one of the Humvees pulled the bolt back on his fifty-caliber to cycle the first round on the belt. I thought for a moment that this was it. That Akers was going to make a stand. And if so, I could sit here and watch Jocelyn as she died, caught in a hail of bullets. I could see her head though the back window of the car.

I wanted desperately to get out, run up, and pull her out and back to safety. But I knew there was no chance. Any effort in that direction would trigger the end. I looked at Herman. He was grinding his teeth, his hand buried in the pocket of his coat, underneath the flak jacket. I knew what was there, the .45 pistol he had taken from the trunk of his car. If the MPs knew he had it, they would take it away from him in a heartbeat. But they didn't, and Herman wasn't telling them.

Chapter 27

AKERS PRESSED THE accelerator and headed up the road. There was no need to hurry. He watched in the mirror as the parade of military vehicles sealed off the road behind him, the highway to hell.

He watched the mirror as the slow caravan of red kept coming. And there, lost in the confusion and chaos, the face of the woman sitting in the seat behind him. She seemed serene. Or perhaps it was just the effects of ether. The fact was, she was the only thing of value left in the car, and Akers knew it. He could use her as a shield. Akers knew that it might prolong the outcome, but it wouldn't change it. He wasn't even sure he wanted to use her in that way. The woman who only a short time earlier he was ready to kill had somehow softened him. Whether she realized it or not, she had reached something deep inside him, something he thought was dead. He looked at her in the mirror once more, assumed she was out of it, and said: "Sweetheart. I'm sorry about all of this. It seems that somehow I've lost my way."

"I know that," said Joselyn.

"How long . . ."

"Have I been awake?" she asked. "Long enough to know it's over. You know we all get lost at one time or another. Maybe now is the time to stop and try to find your way back."

"It's too late for that."

"It's never too late."

"You saw what's in the trunk," he told her. "And there's more you don't know about."

"You killed your wife," said Joselyn.

"How did you know?"

"I guessed, earlier today. Some things you said. I knew you were running from something. What of the children?" she asked.

"No, I could never do that," he told her.

They continued to roll slowly down the road, around a bend, for a moment out of the glaring headlights of the parade following them.

"But I was ready to do it to you. You know that."

"But you didn't."

"I didn't have time."

"I don't believe you."

"Why do you say that? You know I would have."

"You could have killed me in the room or here in the car. You had plenty of time and ample opportunity. Instead, you chose to put me to sleep twice. Why?"

He thought for a moment, then finally said: "I don't know."

"I do. I don't think you wanted to kill me."

"If you're trying to save my soul, don't bother," said Akers. "It was lost long ago. And don't try to analyze me."

"I won't"

"No more talk," he said. "There isn't much time."

He took his foot off the gas and allowed the car to roll to a gentle stop. End of the road, middle of nowhere. In front of them loomed the grey walls of the old Spanish mission. Two Humvees with machine guns on top were positioned in front of it. The vented muzzles of the big guns were directed at their car.

"I never got my pictures," she told him.

"Sorry," he said. "Maybe next time. You should come with someone else," he told her. "I was never fit company. Not for a lady like you."

"You shouldn't run yourself down," she said. There was no way she could bring him back from the depths, and Joselyn knew it. Some things are irredeemable, at least in our own minds. And Cameron Akers had gone well past that point.

His gaze wandered up the weathered brick walls to the stark twin crosses on the roof of the old structure. For a man whose entire adult life had been a constant battle between good and evil, right and wrong, he wanted desperately to believe. After all, he was one of the good guys. He had to believe that; otherwise, what was the point? And yet if he was good, if he was on the side of the angels, how was it that he had come to commit so many evil acts?

He turned off the engine, then reached over and took hold of the handle of the Ka-Bar knife. He pulled it from its sheath.

"I want you to open your door and step out of the car very slowly," he told her. "Don't make any sudden moves. Some of those kids out there are gonna be pretty jumpy. Probably never had their finger on the trigger in a situation like this."

"What about you?" she said.

"I'll be right behind you."

"I have a better idea. Why don't you put the knife down. Roll down your window and put your hands out where they can see them. Give yourself up."

"No."

"This isn't going to end well. You know that."

"It's gonna be fine. Now just do as I say."

"I'm not sure I can stand," she told him. "My legs are a little shaky. You did a number on me with the chloroform."

"It was the only time I had my way with you since we left San Diego."

Joselyn smiled. The fear drained away. The calm of his voice in the face of impending violence, the two of them alone in the car, silhouetted in the headlights with guns trained on them humanized him in a way she had not seen before. She realized what it was. The image of Cameron Akers in his natural state.

"Don't worry, I'll help you," he told her.

Chapter 28

HERMAN NOW HAS the .45 out of his pocket, clutched in his hand. I look at him and shake my head. If he shoots Akers, the MPs are likely to unload on him. He's going to get himself shot.

We're out of the vehicle now, and I move forward toward the two MPs in the lead. One of them tells me to stay back. I ignore him. He has both hands up, holding the pistol and trying to steady it in order to get a bead on Akers. Before he can even think about it, Akers hoists Joselyn out of the backseat and directly into the line of fire.

I step in front of the MP so he can't shoot. He tells me to get out of the way. Herman is right behind me.

We keep inching forward until we are out ahead of the two MPs with their drawn pistols. Akers is now no more than twenty feet away. One of the officers is screaming at me, telling me to get back behind the line. A sniper on the roof of the mission is taking aim at the back of Akers's head. "Tell him to hold off," I yell. I can hear them behind me, whispering into the com system for the sniper to hold his fire. If they shoot Akers, and the car is wired, we could all go up.

"Mr. Akers . . ." I yell

"Tell you what, you call me Cam, I'll call you Paul." He steadies Joselyn on her feet and holds her with one arm around her waist. But he doesn't put the knife to her throat. "You're a lucky guy, Paul. You've got a very nice lady here. I hope you appreciate her."

"It's over," I tell him. "Why don't you put the knife down?"

"I take it you found my wife."

"Your children are fine." I would rather talk about something more positive. "They're going to need a father. You should think about that. They love you."

"You think they're still going to love me when they find out what I did to their mother."

"That's a question only they can answer. You need to ask them."

"Give it up," he says.

"It was good that you cared enough about the kids."

"You mean that I didn't murder them?"

"That may sound funny, but it's one hell of a consolation," I tell him.

"What do I get for that? The lawyer's housekeeping seal of approval? You keep talking, I'm gonna cut my own throat," he says.

"He's not going to hurt anyone," says Jocelyn. "He's done. Put down the knife. Please," she pleads with him.

"Joselyn, stop!" I tell her. "Just please be quiet."

"Don't tell her what to do!" says Akers. "The lady has good instincts. It's just that her timing's a little off. She's too late."

I look at her, wondering if he's drugged her. It's obvious she's having trouble standing.

"There is no sense killing another innocent person," I tell him. "Isn't your wife enough?"

"That's not a good argument, counselor. She wasn't innocent. She kicked me out of my own house and kept me from my children."

"This is pointless," says Joselyn. "He's not going to kill me. He could have done it a dozen times today, and he didn't."

"Be quiet," says Akers.

"Why don't you just put it down?" she tells him.

"No."

"What about the car? Is it wired," I ask.

"For what?" says Joselyn.

"Don't answer them," says Akers.

"Explosives."

"No," she says.

"How would she know?" he says. "Fact is, there's a surprise in the trunk,"

"What's that?"

"Open it and find out."

"There are no explosives," says Joselyn. "The car belongs to another man. He is no threat. I'm telling you."

"Tell that to the cadaver in the trunk," says Akers. "I think this has gone about as far as it can." He leans up close into her ear, and says: "I'm sorry it has to end this way."

"No!" Joselyn screams.

I watch as he releases his arm from around her waist. With his right foot he sweeps her legs out from under her. Joselyn goes to the ground, deadweight. An instant later, Akers steps over her and advances on me with the knife. He closes to maybe ten feet.

Herman raises the pistol, but before he can fire, MPs shoot off several rounds. They hit Akers dead center in the chest. Half a second later, his head explodes in a ball of red mist, followed an instant later by the explosion from the sniper's rifle on the mission roof behind him. Suicide by MP. Akers's lifeless body drops to the sandy soil, his tortured soul lifted skyward in an earthy cloud of dust.

Chapter 29

THE ECHO FROM the rifle is still bouncing off the hills as I step around Akers's body in the dirt and run toward Joselyn on the ground behind him. She is shaking, almost convulsive, crying, tears flowing down both cheeks as I lift her into my arms and cradle her head on my shoulder.

"Easy," I tell her. "It's all right. It's over."

"Why . . ." She tries to speak but cannot.

Behind me, several of the MPs are huddled over Akers's body, none of them making any effort at resuscitation. The wound to his head is massive and obviously fatal. I turn to steer Joselyn's gaze away from the gruesome scene and slowly walk her around the gathering crowd toward one of the Humvees. She is still unsteady on her feet.

Herman sees us and quickly talks to an officer, who immediately orders one of the drivers to get us out of there. Two minutes later, we're on the road headed to the base dispensary, where Joselyn can recover and medics can take a look at her.

TWO MONTHS LATER, and Joselyn is still seeing a therapist. She has nightmares of the events on the base, a contagion perhaps of the disease that ultimately took the life of Cameron Akers as well as his two victims. The precise trigger, what set him off, causing him to kill his wife, we may never know, but the underlying condition was clear. According to a recent study by the Department of Veterans Affairs, almost once every hour a military veteran commits suicide. Beyond this are the active-duty suicides. According to statistics released by the military, active-duty suicides reached a record of 349, nearly one a day, over a recent one-year period. Strange as it may seem, this is a lower rate than the general population, whose rate is on the rise. It seems we are a nation of suicides. Nonetheless, for every veteran killed by the enemy, twenty-five take their own lives. Many of these are the result of depression and mental illness.

Figures show that there are more than 2.3 million American military veterans from the Iraq-Afghanistan wars, and of these, 20 percent suffer from posttraumatic stress disorder. There is no question in my mind but that Cameron Akers was one of these, and suffer he did, along with his wife, his children, and others who came in contact with him.

As for his children, they are now living with Allyson Akers's family, cared for and loved.

Joselyn and I seem to have acquired a new beginning from all of this. My practice is on the edge, but the good news is that the two of us are closer than before. It is strange to say, but the nearness of her, not to Akers but to the sickness that consumed him, has given us new life—like a near miss with cancer. It makes the separation when she is away for business more difficult to bear, but as always, she needs her space and her own goals in life, and we need each other's love.

Keep reading for an excerpt from

The Enemy Inside

**the next installment in Steve Martini's
thrilling Paul Madriani series**

**Coming in hardcover May 2015
From William Morrow**

Chapter 1

"I SAW IT in the paper this morning," says Harry. "Sounds like a barbecue without the tailgate. Driver flambéed behind the wheel in her car. If you like, I'll take it off your hands, but why would we want the case?" To Harry it sounds like a dog.

I ignore him. "The cops are still trying to identify the victim," I tell him.

Harry Hinds is my partner of more than twenty years, Madriani & Hinds, Attorneys at Law, Coronado near San Diego. Business has been thin of late. For almost two years we had been on the run, hiding out from a Mexican killer named Liquida who was trying to punch holes in us with a stiletto. This is apparently what passes for business in the world of narco-fueled revenge. And the man wasn't even a client.

For a while, after it ended and Liquida was dead, the

papers were full of it. Harry and I, along with Herman Diggs, our investigator, became local celebrities.

Everything was fine until the FBI stepped in. They announced publicly that they were giving us a citizen's award for cooperation with law enforcement. For a firm of criminal defense lawyers, this was the kiss of death, Satan giving Gabriel a gold star.

Referrals on cases dried up like an Egyptian mummy. Everywhere we went, other lawyers who knew us stopped shaking our hands and began giving us hugs, frisking us to see which of us was wearing the wire. Harry and I are no longer welcome at defense bar luncheons unless we go naked.

"You look like hell," says Harry.

"Thanks."

"Just to let you know, a beard does not become you."

I have not shaved since yesterday morning. "I was up at four this morning meeting with our client at the county lockup in the hospital."

"You or him?" he asks.

"What?"

"Which one of you was being treated?" says Harry.

"I look that bad?"

He nods.

"Alex Ives, twenty-six, arrested for DUI. A few bruises. No broken bones," I tell him.

"That still doesn't answer my question. Why are we taking the case? Is there a fee involved?"

"He's a friend of Sarah's," I tell him.

"Ahh . . ." He nods slowly as if to say, "We are now reduced to this."

Sarah is my daughter. She is mid-twenties going on forty and has a mother complex for troubled souls. She seems to have been born with a divining rod for knowing the naturally correct thing to do in any situation. Not just social etiquette, but what is right. Sarah lacks the gene that afflicts so many of the young with poor judgment. You might call her old-fashioned. I choose to call her wise. For this, I am blessed. For the same reason, when she asks a favor, I would very likely come to question my own judgment if I said no.

"The kid didn't call me," I tell Harry. "He called Sarah. Apparently they've known each other since high school."

"So what did he have to say?" says Harry. "This client of ours?"

"Says he's sorry, and he's scared."

"That's it?"

"The sorry part. The rest hung over him like a vapor. You'd think he'd never seen concrete walls before." Alex Ives seemed to be dying of sleep deprivation, and still the fear was dripping off him like an icicle. "Said he'd never been arrested before."

"What else?"

"Apart from that, he can't remember a thing."

"Well, at least he remembered that part. Hope he told the cops the same story." Harry looks at me over the top of his glasses, cheaters that he wears mostly for reading. "You believe him? Or do you think maybe he was just that juiced? If he's telling the truth, with that kind of memory loss he probably blew a zero-point-three on the Breathalyzer."

"He was unconscious at the scene. We won't get the blood alcohol report until this afternoon. Cops said they smelled alcohol on him."

"And, of course, while they were treating him and he was unconscious, they sank their fangs into his neck and drew blood," says Harry.

"A passing motorist pulled him from his car and away from the flames. Otherwise we wouldn't even have him. Everything inside both cars was toast."

"Thank God for small favors." Sarcasm is Harry's middle name.

"It looks like Ives T-boned the other vehicle at an intersection, a dirt road and a two-lane highway east of town out in the desert. Way the hell out, according to the cops. McCain Valley Road."

"He lives out there?"

"No. He lives in town. A condo in the Gas Lamp District."

"What was he doing way out there? That's fifty miles as the crow flies," says Harry.

I shake my head. "Says he doesn't know. The last thing he remembers is being at a party up north near Del Mar, about seven thirty last evening, and then nothing."

"Was he drinking at this party?" says Harry.

"Says he had one drink."

"How big was the glass? Anybody with him? I mean, to vouch for this one-drink theory."

I shake my head. "He says he was alone."

"Let's see if I've got this . . . unconscious at the scene, smells of alcohol and the other driver is dead. And now he can't remember anything, except for the fact that he had only one drink. I'd say we got the wrong client. Why couldn't Sarah know the cinder in the other car? Her blood kin at least will have a good civil case." What Harry means is damages against our guy. "Tell me he has insurance and a valid license." Harry doesn't want to be stuck fending off a wrongful death case with no coverage while jousting with a prosecutor over hard time for vehicular manslaughter.

I nod. "He has insurance and a license that hasn't been revoked as far as I know. They ran a rap sheet and found no priors. So he doesn't look to be a habitual drunk."

"That could mean that he's just been lucky up to now." Harry is the essential cynic.

"He could be lying about what he remembers. Like I say, he's scared."

"He should be," says Harry. "He could be facing anywhere from four to six years in the pen."

In a death case, prosecutors will invariably push for the upper end. MADD, Mothers Against Drunk Drivers, has sensitized district attorneys and judges who have to stand for election to the realities of politics. By the same token, the other party is dead and you can bet the prosecutor who tries the case will be reminding the jury and the judge of this fact at every opportunity.

"Anything by way of an accident report?" says Harry.

"Not out yet," I tell him.

"What does our client remember about this party he went to?"

"According to Ives, he was invited to the gig by some girl he met at work. The scene was a big house, swimming pool, lots of people, music, an open bar, but he can't remember the address."

"Of course not," says Harry.

"He said he'd recognize the place if he saw it again. The street address was on a note that he had in his wallet. Along with the girl's name and phone number."

"So he'd never met this girl before?"

"No. And he can't remember her name."

"She must have made a deep impression," says Harry. "Still, her name will be on the note in the wallet. The cops have it, I assume?" says Harry.

"No. As a matter of fact, they don't. I checked. They got his watch, some cash he had in his pocket, and a graduation ring from college."

"That's it?"

"They figure the wallet must have been lost on the seat of the car, or else he dropped it somewhere. . . ."

"So, assuming this note existed, it probably got torched in the fire." Harry finishes the thought for me. "You can bet the cops will be looking for it. If our boy was falling-down drunk when he left the party, there will be lots of people who saw him, witnesses," says Harry, "but not for our side. Without the wallet, how did the cops ID him if, as you say, he was unconscious?"

"Fingerprints. Ives had a temp job with a defense contractor a few years ago, a software company under contract to the navy. His prints were on file."

"And the girl who invited him, did he see her at the party?"

"He says she never showed, or at least he doesn't remember," I tell him.

"Convenient." Harry is thinking that there was no party, that Ives got drunk somewhere else, maybe a bar, and doesn't want to fess up because he knows there were witnesses who can testify as to his lack of sobriety. Harry goes silent for a moment as he thinks. Then the ultimate question: "How are we getting paid for this? Does our client have anything that passes for money?"

"No." I watch his arched eyebrows collapse before I add: "But his parents do. They own a large aviation servicing company at the airport. Quite well off, from what I understand. And they love their son. I met them at the hospital. Lovely people. You'll like them."

"I already do." Harry smiles, a broad affable grin. "Thank Sarah for the referral," he says.

Chapter 2

HERE IS THE mystery. Alex Ives's blood alcohol report showed up at our office this morning. And surprise, Ives was not over the legal limit. In fact, he wasn't even close. In California, the threshold is set at a 0.08 percent blood alcohol level. Ives barely tilted the meter at 0.01. You would probably show a higher blood alcohol level hosing out your mouth with some mouthwash. There is no question concerning the accuracy of the test. They drew blood. It is beginning to look as if Ives's story of having only one drink is true. He may not have even finished it.

In the world of simple citations for a DUI, driving under the influence, that would probably be the end of the case. The prosecutor would dump it or charge Ives with a lesser-included offense, speeding or weaving in the lane if they saw him driving. But the charge of vehicular manslaughter has them looking deeper. The cops are now back, burning Bunsens in their lab looking for drugs. The chemical tests for these take a lot longer. So we wait.

Harry and I have delivered the good news and the bad news to Ives in one of the small conference rooms at the county lockup.

"You sure you weren't on any medications?" I ask him.

"Nothing," says Ives.

We are trying to prep for a bail hearing tomorrow morning, looking for anything that might stand in the way of springing him from the county's concrete abode.

Ives looks at us from across the table. Sandy haired, big bright blue eyes, well over six feet, a tall wiry rail of a kid, and scared. Jimmy Stewart in his youth unburdening his soul to two hapless angels.

"If there is anything in the blood they will find it," says Harry.

"I don't do drugs," says Ives.

"Good boy," says Harry.

"What do we have on the other driver?" I look at my partner. Harry hasn't had time to read all the reports. They have been coming in in bits and pieces over a couple of days now. "Any alcohol in her body? Could be *she* was drinking."

"If she was, it went up in the flames," says Harry. He is master of documents this afternoon, a growing file spread out on the metal table in front of him. "According to the accident report, the victim's name was Serna, first name Olinda. Forty-seven years old. Out-of-state license, driving a rental car. . . ."

"What did you say her name was?" says Ives.

Harry glances at him, then looks down at the page again. "Serna, Olinda Serna. I guess that's how you'd pronounce it."

"Can't be," says Ives.

"What are you talking about?" I ask.

"Can't be her," says Ives.

"Can't be who?"

"Serna," he says.

I glance at Harry who has the same stagestruck expression as I do.

"Are you telling us you knew her?" says Harry.

"No, no. It must be somebody else. Maybe the same name," says Ives.

Harry gives me a look as if to say, "How many Olindas do you know?"

"Assuming it's her, I didn't really know her. Never met her. I just know the name. It's a story we've been working on at the *Gravesite*. My job," says Ives.

Harry is now sitting bolt upright in the chair. "Explain!"

"We've been working on this story close to a year now. Major investigation," he says. "And I recognize the name. Assuming it's the same person."

"Where was this person from?" asks Harry. "This person in your story. Where did she live? What city?"

"It would be somewhere around Washington, D.C., if it's her."

Harry is looking at the report, flips one page, looks up and says: "Is Silver Spring, Maryland, close enough?"

"The cops never told you who the victim was?" I ask Ives.

"No, I didn't know until just now. No idea," he says.

"Do you know what this other woman, the one in your story, did for a living?" Harry looks at him.

"She was a lawyer," says Alex.

"Mandella, Harbet, Cain, and Jenson?" says Harry.

Ives's face is all big round eyes at this moment, his Adam's apple bobbing.

"Well, I guess if you have to kill a lawyer, you may as well kill a big corporate one," says Harry.

According to the police report, the cops found business cards in the victim's purse, what was left of it. They ID'ed her from those and the VIN number on the burned-out car that was traced back to the rental agency.

Mandella is one of the largest law firms in the country. It has offices in a dozen cities in the Americas, Europe, and Asia. The minute the ashes cool from the Arab Spring, you can bet they will be back there as well. They practice law the same way the US military fights its battles, with overwhelming force, cutting-edge weapons, and surprise flanking power plays. If their clients can't win on the law, they will go to Congress and change it.

The multinational businesses that are not on their client list are said not to be worth having. One of their long-dead managing partners, it is rumored, got the feuding Arab clans to put down their guns long enough to set up OPEC, the world oil cartel, at which point the Arabs stopped robbing camel caravans and started plundering the industrialized West. If you believe Mandella's PR, lawyers from the firm secured the foreign flag rights for Noah's ark. They would glaze the words "Super Lawyers" on the glass doors to their offices, but who needs it when the brass plaques next to it show a list of partners including four retired members of the US Senate and one over-the-hill Supreme Court Justice. The finger of God is said to be painted on the ceiling of their conference rooms, franchise rights for which they acquired when Jehovah evicted their client, Adam, from the Garden of Eden.

"Listen, you have to believe me," says Ives. "I had no idea. I don't remember anything about the accident or anything about that night. Nothing. I don't remember the other car. I don't remember hitting it. I don't remember getting in my car to drive. The last thing I remember is going to the party, having a drink, and then nothing." He looks at us for a moment, to Harry and then back to me. "I mean . . . I know it looks bad. The fact I even knew who she was. But I never met her."

"It appears that you ran into her at one point," says Harry. Bad joke. "You have to admit, it's one hell of a co-incidence. Let's hope the cops don't know."

Harry and I are thinking the same thing. The police may change their theory of the case if they find out there was any connection between Ives and the victim before the accident.

"Tell us what this story is about," says Harry. "The one involving Serna."

"Oh, I can't do that," says Ives.

"What?" says Harry.

"Not without an OK from my editor."

"An OK from your editor?" says Harry. "Do you understand what you're facing here? If the cops get wind of any involvement between you and the victim, they are going to start turning over rocks looking for evidence of intentional homicide. Depending on what they find, you won't be looking at manslaughter any longer but murder. Was there any bad blood between you and her?"

"Not on my part. It was just a story. Nothing personal," says Ives.

"What is this story about?"

"You don't really think I killed her on purpose?"

"For my part, I don't. But I can't vouch for the D.A.," says Harry. "So why don't you fill us in."

"It's big. It's a very big story. At this point there are a lot of leads. What we need is confirmation."

"Confirmation of what?" Harry is getting hot.

"That's what I can't tell you," says Ives. "It's not my story. I don't have any personal stake in it. That's what I'm saying. I didn't have any reason to harm Serna. I never met her. She was a name. That's all."

"But she was involved?" I ask.

"Her name kept popping up during the investigation," says Ives.

Alex is what passes for an investigative reporter in the age of digital news. The changing tech world has dislocated everything from journalism to jukeboxes. It has untethered us from the world we thought we knew and left us to swim in a sea of uncertainty. Like primitive natives, we are constantly dazzled by shiny new stuff, smartphones that respond to voice commands and mobile hot spots the size of a thimble that connect us to the universe.

But like the native jungles of the New World, the industries in which we work may disappear tomorrow, victims of the shiny new stuff, the treasures that have seduced us. Where newspapers once existed, now there are blog sites. More nimble, faster, some of them blunt-edged partisan weapons for dismantling a republic. Alex works for one of these, a blog site headquartered in Washington. He is their West Coast correspondent.

"I'm not sure how much I can tell you. We've been working on it for about a year now. Mostly in D.C., but also out here on the coast. It's the reason I know her name."

"If you want us to represent you," says Harry, "you're going to have to trust us."

"I do. But you have to understand the story is not mine, it belongs to the *Gravesite*." Ives is talking about the *Washington Gravesite*, the digitized scandal sheet owned by Tory Graves, Ives's boss and the purveyor of the hottest political dirt since the days of Drew Pearson and Jack Anderson. What TMZ is to celebrity news and entertainment gossip, the *Washington Gravesite* is to those who work in politics. It parcels out breaking news to the various cable stations, which feed upon it depending on their particular partisan political bias. It is unclear how Graves makes his money, whether he gets paid for exclusive stories or is funded by various interest groups with an ax to grind. Either way he seems to be surviving in what is by any measure a political snake pit of Olympian proportions.

"Did you ever talk to Serna, interview her, have any direct contact with her at all?" asks Harry.

Ives is shaking his head.

"Did you communicate with her in any way?" I ask.

"No. And I can't tell you anything beyond that, not until I talk to my editor."

Harry and I look at each other. I give Ives a big sigh, shrug my shoulders, and slowly shake my head. "We're just trying to help you."

"I know you are and I appreciate it," says Ives. "But I can't talk about my work. That's confidential. It's off-limits."

"Let's hope the court agrees," says Harry. "But I can tell you it won't."

"Let's leave it for the moment," I tell him. "I assume your parents are good for the bail bond?"

"I think so. How much do you think it'll be?"

"No way to be certain until we get in front of the judge. It's a bailable offense, at least at the moment. But the D.A. will probably try to up the ante. Make it expensive. Have you done any recent international travel?"

"For work," he says.

"How long ago and how often?"

"Europe, twice in the last year."

"Where?" says Harry.

"I went to Switzerland with my boss, Tory Graves."

"We can assume Serna wasn't into chocolates," says Harry. "Watches? Rolexes?" He looks at Ives. "Banking!"

The kid's face flushes. He looks up at Harry.

"Bingo. Well, we can't put him on the stand," says Harry. "They won't need a lie detector to test his veracity. Just measure the movement of his Adam's apple. I hope you don't play poker, son. If you ever take it up, try to sit under the table."

"You can be sure they will want your passport until this is over," I tell him. "As for bail, you have a job and contacts in the community. That's a plus. Superior Court bail schedule says a hundred-thousand-dollar bond for a death case involving DUI. That means you or your parents have to put up ten percent, ten grand."

Ives shakes his head, looks down at the table. "I suspect my parents can raise it. But I'll want to pay them back."

"Of course."

"And your fees," he says.

"Let's not worry about that right now." Harry gives me a dirty look.

"What about the girl, the one you say you met who invited you to the party? What can you tell us about her?"

"Not much," he says. "Only met her the one time."

"How did you meet her?" says Harry.

"Let me think. I guess it was about noon. I was out in the plaza in front of my office trying to figure where to go to grab a bite. This girl came up to me, real cute, you know, and she asked me for directions."

"To where?"

"I don't remember exactly."

"Go on," I tell him.

"It must have been somewhere close. I mean, she didn't come out of a car at the curb or anything. Not that I saw anyway. So I assume she was on foot."

"Was she alone?" I ask.

"As far as I could tell, she was."

"But you don't know where she was going?" says Harry.

Alex shakes his head.

"And then what?" I ask.

"We got to talking. She had a great smile. Said there was a party at some rich guy's house that night. She said she was gonna be there. It might be fun. Said she was allowed to invite some friends. Would I like to go? What could I say? Beautiful girl. I had nothing going on that night. I said sure. She gave me the information . . ."

"How?" I ask. "How did she give you the information?"

"A note," he says. "It had the address and a phone number. The address was the location of the party. She said the number was her cell phone in case I got lost. It wouldn't have mattered. I went to call her when she didn't show and my phone was dead."

That means we can't subpoena the cell carrier to try and triangulate the location of the house where the party took place.

"All I can remember is it was someplace up near Del Mar. Big house in a ritzy neighborhood. I remember it had a big pool, great big oval thing. I might recognize it if I saw it again. The problem is, you use this high-tech stuff, GPS, you tend to rely on it and you don't remember anything because you don't have to."

Alex is right. How many of us can remember telephone numbers for friends or family? We push a button and it replaces our brains.

"I loaded the address into the GPS in the car and I didn't pay any attention. I just followed the verbal directions. It took me right to the front door," he says.

And of course Alex's car, which he borrowed from his parents' company, was charred in the accident. Its GPS is toast. I make a note to check and see if we can access the information from its provider, OnStar or NavSat or one of the others.

"Oh, there was one more thing," says Alex. "She gave me a name. Some guy. She said that if anyone stopped me at the door, I was to tell them I was to be seated at this guy's table."

"What was the name?" says Harry.

Ives looks at us, first to Harry and then to me. Shakes his head. "I can't remember," he says. "Bender or Billings, something like that. I think it started with a *B*."

"This note, with the address on it. Did she write it down or did you?" I ask.

He thought about it for a moment. "Come to think," he says, "neither one of us did. She already had it written out. She just handed it to me."

"Didn't you think that was a little strange?" says Harry. "A girl you just met handing out invitations to a party to strangers on the street?"

"She looked like the kind of girl who would have rich friends," says Ives. "When I got to the party, I realized I wasn't exactly dressed for it," he says.

"What do you mean?" says Harry.

"I mean, there were guys there wearing tuxes, women in expensive dresses and a lot of jewels. And they were all older. Gray hair everywhere I looked. I felt out of place, like maybe she should have warned me. I went looking for her. My first thought was maybe there was a younger crowd somewhere in the back. It was a big place, a lot of ground in the yard. Chinese lanterns lighting everything up. She was right about one thing. Whoever owned the place was part of the one percent," he says. "A lot of money.

"When I didn't see her or anyone our age, I decided to leave. That's when he came by."

"Who?" says Harry.

"The waiter with a tray of drinks. They didn't have any beer, but they had champagne. I took one glass, and that's it. That's all I can remember until I woke up in the hospital."

"Do you remember what he looked like, the waiter?"

"Not a clue. Didn't even look. It was crowded. There were people everywhere. I grabbed the glass and that was it."

"Do you remember what the girl looked like?" I ask him.

"Yeah. You couldn't forget her. Asian. Beautiful face. Great smile. Long straight black hair down to the middle of her back. Dark eyes. Bronze skin. About this tall." Ives puts his hand flat on edge as if drawing a line across his upper body about nipple high.

"What are you saying, about five five, five six?" I ask.

"Yeah, I'd say that's about right."

"Was she slender, heavy? How was she built?"

"Yeah." Ives gives me a kind of quick sheepish grin,

the college jock. "I'd say she was pretty well built. You know what I mean?"

"Tell us." Commander Lust, Harry wants all the details.

"Well, you know . . . showing some good cleavage. It was a nice sunny day. Summertime. A lot of the women, secretaries, come out of the buildings into the plaza showing a lotta thigh, short skirts. Hers was right up there. You couldn't miss it," he says. "As I remember, she was wearing a blue print dress of some kind, tight, a lot of curves, all in the right places, and . . . oh, yeah, she had a tattoo."

"Yes?" I look at him.

"It looked like the tail of a dragon, blue and red; it was a colorful thing. It was on the inside of her left thigh. Fairly high up. By the way she was dressed I could only see the bottom part of it. But you could bet I wanted to see more."

"Looks to me like she was waiting for you," says Harry. "Everything but a pole with a lure on it."

"With that kind of a lure, she didn't need the pole," I tell him.

This thought is not lost on Ives. "I've wondered about that."

"Do you think you could have been drugged at the party?" I ask.

"I've thought about that, too," he says. "I guess I'm pretty stupid. But they didn't rob me. They didn't take any money, my watch, my phone, nothing."

"Any idea how you got way out to the accident site?" says Harry.

"I'm not entirely certain where that was," he says.

"Try sixty miles out of town," I say. "East, out in the desert."

He shakes his head. "It doesn't make any sense. You think I could have driven all the way out there, gotten into an accident, totaled two cars, killed somebody, and not remember anything?"

"I don't know," I tell him. "The only connection from what you're telling us is your job, this story you were working on."

"She was part of it," says Ives. He's talking about Serna.

I sit there looking at him, waiting for him to fill the nervous void. "Just give me some clue," I tell him.

"In general terms?" he says. "What it's always about when it comes to politics and business. What do they say? Follow the money. What the Swiss bankers call Ben and Bin."

"What does that mean? Ben and Bin?" says Harry.

"In international financial circles, Ben is a hundred-dollar bill. Bin is a five-hundred-euro note," says Ives. "Follow the money. It's always about the money." Then he suddenly gives us a distant stare as if he's looking right through the cement wall in the cubicle. "That's it!"

"What?" says Harry.

"Her name. The girl. The one who invited me to the party. Now I remember. Her name was Ben."

CLETUS PROFFIT, THE managing partner of the Mandella law firm, looks a lot like one of the characters from an old Hitchcock movie. It was the cadaverous assassin in a tux, brandishing a pistol at the Albert Hall in *The Man Who Knew Too Much*. The title, if you put it in the present tense, would have made a fitting moniker for Proffit's business card. Though at the moment he was more worried about what he didn't know.

"Clete," as his associates call him, was an up-from-the-bootstraps lawyer, a graduate of Harvard Law, originally out of the Midwest, a man who kept climbing his entire life and never looked back. His father had been a store clerk in a small town in Iowa, a fact that Proffit spent most of his life trying to forget. You could mark the significant waypoints in his career by the scandals he had sidestepped and the bodies he had climbed over along the way.

He had spent a few years in government, but never as a civil servant. Clete always believed in starting near the top; undersecretary of defense in the waning days of one administration and special assistant to the president in another. He was rumored to be on a short list for a Cabinet spot, perhaps attorney general, as soon as his party was back in power. Poster boy for the revolving door but always, in the end, back to the firm. It was the chair that was always there whenever the music stopped.

Quiet, in the same way a leopard is before he jumps you, Proffit was always the last to speak on any controversy at a meeting. Not because he was shy but because he was searching for qualities of leadership in others. Leading from behind was the best way to identify competitors so you could sink your canines into the back of their neck while they were still moving forward.

The firm's headquarters were located in Los Angeles, though Proffit spent much of his time skipping like a stone off the stratosphere between there and Washington, D.C. He had spent too much of his life getting his hand on the spigot of power to let go now. Increasingly, that elixir and the people who were under its delirious effects resided in Washington, as did the mounting threat to Proffit's future and his continued leadership of the firm: Olinda Serna.

"She's gone now. You can relax," said Fischer.

"There's everything to worry about." Proffit froze Fischer with an icy glance. "You don't kill a vampire in a car crash. That requires a silver bullet or a wooden stake. Take your pick. And even then you can't be sure she hasn't left toxic entrails behind." He was curious as to details of how she died. According to the sparse reports, the accident happened on a deserted road some miles from San Diego. What was she doing there? He had already told his secretary back in L.A. to get a copy of the accident report as soon as it was prepared.

Proffit hated Serna in a way that left its mark on the core of his very being. They both prayed at the altar of progressive politics, and in a public fashion that no one could miss. Proffit did his time on the board of the ACLU and took his share of high-profile pro bono cases for the poor, minorities, the oppressed, and every other needy group.

Serna wrapped herself in the body armor of women's rights as protection against the male lawyers who dominated the firm. She served on the board of directors of several women's organizations and carried the banner of liberation like a cattle prod. She poked Proffit in the ass with it enough times to remind him that electricity could hurt. The last thing you ever wanted was an injured woman coming out of the woodwork screaming sexual harassment when your name was on the short list for power player of the week in a rising administration. To those in the glass bowl of power it was all a matter of perspective. If your heart was in the right place and your behind was on the correct side of the political divide, such claims would wither in a desert of disregard. But woe unto those in the wrong party, or worse, who had made enemies in the activist camp. For them the ninth circle of hell would provide a refreshing interlude from the pounding they would take before Senate committees in confirmation hearings. Tales of pubic hairs on cans of cola were mild compared to the nuclear crap that would rain down on you from the cloud and the Internet, which had a habit of breeding other victims and cloning new complaints. All of this could be yours if you fell into the cross hairs of the wrong activist group, something that Olinda Serna could guarantee if you got on her wrong side.

"You worry too much," said Fischer.

"Is that right? Tell me," said Proffit, "how much do we really know about what she was involved in, here at the firm, I mean? Do you know?"

Fischer stood there, his lower jaw beginning to quiver with disclaimers. "I just meant . . ."

"I know what you meant. She was running her own secret empire within the firm. You know it and I know it. What we don't know are the details of what she was into."

"As I recall, you didn't want to know," said Fischer.

"That was when she was alive," said Proffit.

Cyril Fischer was Proffit's number two, managing-partner-in-waiting at the firm, and a man who Proffit knew would never get there. He lacked the instincts for survival as well as the searing coals in the belly that fired ambition. This was the reason Proffit kept him around. He was useful as a pair of eyes and ears, but he was no threat. Fischer ran the Washington office, at least on paper.

"If she had people on the cuff in Congress that she was paying off, you're damn right I didn't want to know.

If you mean poisoned e-mails from Olinda to keep me in the loop, you're correct. I had no desire to be on that mailing list."

It was the kind of stuff a wily lawyer and pillar of the community like Proffit generally didn't want to know about. He had imagination enough to fill in the blanks. And if Serna got in trouble, Proffit would protect himself like a mobster with at least three or four layers of subordinates to insulate him from accountability. But now that Serna was dead he had no choice. If there were damaging documents lurking in her files, he had to protect the firm, and by extension, himself. They would have to find some lawyerly way to inoculate themselves and disinfect the office.

Serna was the firm's "juice lady," specializing in political law and lobbying—"mother's milk," political money, action committees, and donor lists—the dark side of democracy. She had no personal life, no family, and seemingly no existence outside of the steaming swamp that was Washington and in which she seemed to thrive. For some time now, from what Proffit could see, her ambition had gotten the better of her. She had turned her job into a launching pad in an increasingly obvious campaign to unseat him at the head of the table within the firm.

"I've got two trusted associates and three secretaries auditing her files and checking her e-mails as we speak," said Fischer. "If there's anything there, I'm sure we've got it contained."

This is what Proffit expected. They were looking in all the wrong places. "What I'm worried about you won't find in her files." Proffit knew that anything in her office files, short of hostage notes or blackmail letters, the firm could probably throw a blanket over under attorney-client privilege or lawyer work product and probably make it stick. "That's not the problem."

"What then?" said Fischer.

"Sit down for a minute and let me think."

Fischer wandered toward one of the client chairs across from Proffit's enormous mahogany desk, slumped into the deep cushions, and stared at his boss across the shimmering plate-glass surface.

What troubled Proffit was that Serna was a loner. If she had shot a dozen people in a shopping mall they would have said she fit the profile. Usually in a hurry, irritable, always on her own mission, a cipher you couldn't read if they gave you the code. She was dedicated to her work in the way a zealot is to his ideology. She had her fingers in almost everything the firm handled if it had to do with the gods of politics. She blanketed Congress, the regulatory agencies, and the White House and did it all by herself. At times Proffit was left to wonder if she had cloned herself. If she had posted a sixty-hour day on her billings no one who knew her would have accused her of padding the bill. Her work ethic wasn't the problem. The fact that she had an ambition to match it was.

More to the point, Serna had her own power base outside the firm, mostly friends on Capitol Hill and in the bowels of the administration. She was a registered lobbyist, one of only three in the firm. She either directly or indirectly ladled campaign money on members of the

House and Senate from well-heeled clients, many of them large well-organized trade associations and corporate business groups. It wasn't her money, but as far as the recipients were concerned, it didn't matter. She was on the giving end. Otherwise, it would have been an easy task for Proffit and his supporters in the firm to outflank her, undercut her, and send her packing. The problem was, if they did that, they couldn't be sure of the political or economic fallout.

If deals were made on critical legislation with Serna in the middle and her friends in Congress on the doing end, high-paying clients of the firm might feel more comfortable with her than with Mandella. Especially if they started receiving phone calls or e-mails from Serna's friends in the Capitol. She had come from congressional staff when they hired her, consultant to the Senate Banking Committee. She had a lot of friends there. It was a delicate problem, not one that was easily or quickly dealt with.

"Where did she live?" Proffit looked off into the distance to the side away from Fischer as he asked the question.

"Somewhere in Silver Spring. We have the address in our records."

"Has anybody been over there since the accident? Anybody with a key?" Proffit turned and burned two holes through Fischer with his gaze. He didn't have to wait for an answer. The expression on Fischer's face said it. Fischer hadn't thought about this.

"She wasn't married, had no lovers that we know of. Lived alone, right?"

Fischer nodded. "As far as I know."

"She didn't or I would have known about it," said Proffit.

Fischer didn't ask how. Clete always had his sources.

"If there is anything we should worry about, it's not going to be in her files here at the firm. It's going to be in one of two places," said Proffit. "She may have stashed documents at her house. That includes her home computer, any thumb drives or other portable storage devices, and paper records. Perhaps a safe-deposit box. Did she have one?"

"I don't know."

"The weight of what you don't know could sink us," said Proffit.

"What is it exactly that you're worried about?" asked Fischer. "If you could give me some specifics it might help."

"I'm worried about whatever it is that I don't know," said Proffit. If Serna had been one of their corporate lawyers, even one of their stables of criminal trial lawyers, Proffit wouldn't have been so concerned. It was the nature of her work that scared him, and her ambition. She was in a position to do real damage both to himself and the firm. They were one and the same as far as Proffit was concerned. From what he could see, she was already in the process of doing that damage when she died.

"Who is her next of kin?" he asked.

Fischer shook his head, shrugged a shoulder.

"Well, goddamn it, find out! See if she had a company life insurance policy. If so, there should be a named beneficiary. That may be it. Did she have any other property besides the place in Georgetown? A vacation hideaway where she may have stored documents?"

Again Fischer didn't know. But by now he was taking notes on Post-it slips from the little square holder on Proffit's desk.

"Did she own or rent the place in Georgetown?"

"Owned. I think."

"Well, find out!" said Proffit. "We don't want some nosy landlord traipsing through the place looking at things until we've had a chance to do it ourselves. Did she have anybody else in the firm she trusted, any associates?"

"She wanted to hire an assistant. You said no."

"I know what I said. Was there anybody in the office she confided in?"

"I didn't follow her into the ladies' room, if that's what you mean. Vicki Preebles was her secretary. I assume if she trusted anybody it would have been her."

"Was Preebles upset by the news? Serna's death, I mean?"

"Sure. Wouldn't you be? She wanted to stay and help out, but I told her to take a couple days off. I felt it was the thing to do," said Fischer. "We can wait a respectful period and then debrief her. See what Serna may have told her. If anybody knows anything, I suspect it's her."

"Hmmm."

"And I changed the locks on Serna's office just like you said."

"Good." Proffit thought to himself that if Cyril Fischer ever got disbarred, perhaps he could make a living as a locksmith.

Chapter 4

HER PRINCIPAL VALUE rested not in her ability to kill her victims, though she was proficient in this. Her usefulness flowed from her knowledge of forensic science and, in particular, trace evidence, hair and fibers, minute particles of dirt, pollen, and other microscopic bits of information that could compromise a job. Sometimes she worked alone and sometimes with others to make sure they made no mistakes and left no telltale signs behind.

You could call her a hired mercenary, but of a special kind. She seldom, if ever, worked in a war zone; almost always in developed countries, Western Europe, the first world nations of Asia, the Middle East, and the Americas.

Governments and large corporations hired her because they knew her skills and could afford the price of her services. She spoke several languages, Spanish, Portuguese, French, a smattering of German along with some Russian. Her English, though fluent, if you listened closely, carried a hint of what sounded like a Spanish trill, so that you might mistake her background as Latin American if you didn't know better.

Ana Agirre was Basque, born in the Pyrenees Mountains between France and Spain. Her great-grandfather died in the bombing of Guernica by the Germans in 1937 during the Spanish Civil War, a travesty made famous by Picasso's painting of the same name. Both her father and her mother worked in the Basque underground before the end of the Franco regime and then afterward, part of the ETA, the Basque separatist movement. Her mother died smuggling explosives during an ETA mission in Barcelona. Her father was taken prisoner. She never saw him again. At the time Ana was eight.

Raised by her maternal grandmother, she excelled in school, particularly in science. She graduated from secondary school a year ahead of her classmates. Given her family background and the fear of retaliation by the Spanish government, Ana was sent to college in Paris. She could have taken courses preparing her for medical school or any of the research fields. Instead, she chose criminalistics and later took a job in the crime lab of the Police Nationale, successor to the fabled Sûreté. The French didn't seem to care about her family's background. In fact, some voiced sympathy for the Basque people and their repression under Franco. There she learned and refined her forensic skills.

One would have thought she was on a mission to rehabilitate her family so earnestly did she study, absorbing everything she saw and learned with the zeal of a monk. What she masked was anger, anger at the world for having taken from her the one person in her life who she loved more than life itself, her mother. It was a painful loss, one she could never get over. It came to her in her nightmares, the brilliant flash of fire, the sensation of heat and the shattering sound of the explosion that ripped her mother to pieces. Though she had not witnessed it, she had now seen enough to know what it would have been like, the aftermath of a blast from nearly two kilos, four pounds, of RDX, what the American military called C-4 and the British termed PE-4.

Since she was ten, when she had overheard the whispered conversations of her aunts and uncles in the parlor of her grandmother's house, Ana had known that her mother's coffin, buried in the graveyard of the small church in their village, was empty. There was no body inside. After the blast, police and firefighters had found nothing except bits of charred fabric from her mother's clothing, none of them larger than a few centimeters in size. They determined the source of the explosion from chemical tests at the site.

C-4 was stable. It smelled like motor oil and had the pliable texture of children's clay. But when subjected to heat or the shock produced by a detonator, it would explode with a fiery ear-shattering blast that could level half a city block.

Ana concluded that the bomb must have already been armed with a detonator when whoever made it handed it to her mother. It went off on a quiet street in a Barcelona suburb. The only victims were her mother and Ana, who was left to fend for herself.

She remained with the Paris crime lab for six years

before moving on to a private laboratory that contracted its services to the French military. There she came in contact with representatives for corporate mercenaries who ultimately hired her as an independent contractor. Ana set up her own business. For large fees, sometimes seven figures, she asked no questions and did whatever was asked of her.

Want to burn down a building? Ana would provide you with an incendiary device that would completely consume itself in the flames. Investigators might find the precise location where the fire originated, and if they had sufficient equipment they might sniff out the chemical accelerants. But as to any other evidence, there would be none.

With the money she earned, she purchased a small estate in the hills above the Côte d'Azur in the South of France. There she moved in her grandmother and one of her aging aunts.

While they quietly plied the garden and cooked, Ana traveled the world rendering advice to her corporate and government black-bag clients on how best to sanitize crime scenes, the proper clothing to wear to avoid leaving trace evidence, as well as ways and means to commit undetectable "accidents," almost all of them fatal.

Drug overdoses were often the death of choice if for no other reason than that most people, including the authorities, believed that those who possessed power and wealth might also be possessed by powerful demons. If there was any hint of past drug use, police seldom looked too far in the direction of criminal homicide unless there was some reason to do so. Ana's job was to make sure there was none. This was the kind of subtle refinement that the terrorist community was edging toward as a means of avoiding state-led military retribution whenever possible. If authorities could not prove an intentional killing, it was politically difficult to strike back. Yet the result was the same: an enemy was dead. There was a growing demand for Ana's services, acts that seldom made bold headlines in newspapers and were a blip on the radar of networks and cable news stations.

At times she would render personal service, hands-on expertise, but that always required a substantially higher fee because of the risks involved.

As you might assume, one did not find a listing for Ana Agirre in any phone book or on the World Wide Web. To those who used her services, she was known as "L'architecte de la mort," "the Architect of Death." Jobs were always on a referral basis, from those she trusted and who had used her services previously. One always kept a low profile in her business.

She was lean and strong, five foot nine, a little taller than average, a face you would not notice in a crowd, neither ugly nor fetching, a passing figure no one would ever remember. Ana the Architect did nothing to alter this appearance. She wore no makeup, never donned high heels, and wore no jewelry. Her uniform of choice was a dark sweater-jersey, dark slacks, and black flat rubber-soled deck shoes. Nothing expensive or unique with intricate sole patterns. Her hair was cut short in the fashion of early photographs taken of Audrey Hepburn, something that a victim would have difficulty getting a grip on in a frenzied attempt to fight her off—that is, if they ever saw her coming in the first place. Usually she was so quick and agile that all they would catch was a glimpse through glazed eyes of her back as she walked away. It would likely be the last thing they would ever see.

This morning she was busy reading the online version of the *San Diego Union-Tribune* about an accident near San Diego, California. She sipped her coffee while sitting at one of the outdoor tables at Le Sancerre on the rue des Abbesses in Paris. It was close to the apartment she maintained in the city. She read the scant details on her e-tablet using the portable hot spot in her purse.

"A single fatality, an unidentified woman. The other driver was arrested, believed to have been under the influence of alcohol. The survivor, a man in his twenties, suffered only minor injuries and was taken to a local area hospital for treatment. No identification of the dead driver has been made pending notification of next of kin."

Ana did not know the dead woman's name, but she knew she had been murdered. The French mercenaries, a group of high-tech engineers who had constructed the equipment that caused the accident, had told her to watch the news in this part of California, the area around San Diego.

She had seen only digital pictures of the items, including the large rolling case that was highly unique. It was too big to carry on board an airplane, so it had to be checked. They had marked the case with holograms, making it easily identifiable at baggage claim so that no one would carry it off by mistake. You could just grab it and go. They also sent the specs for the equipment.

This was composed of a computer, its software, and a portable satellite antenna dish capable of overriding most of the electronics and computer-driven safety and other features built into late-model passenger cars.

Ana made a down payment on the equipment because she needed it for a job in Europe. It was a highly lucrative contract involving the untimely accidental death of an executive, the managing partner of a large multinational corporation. If the schedule on the contract for the executive was to be maintained, the gentleman was slated to be dead in two weeks. After that, bad things would happen to the people who hired her.

Ana was anxious to get her hands on the equipment and get the job done. However, the French technicians who built the system insisted on "field-testing" it first before they delivered it to her. They said nothing about a field test at the time she ordered the equipment. Now the stuff was off in California somewhere. According to the French makers, if all went well there would be two dead targets, separate motorists in separate vehicles on a two-lane highway in a rural area east of San Diego. The Frenchmen gave her the date and told her to watch the news. They seemed giddy with excitement.

The news story gave the sorry details. They had not banked on the intervention of a passing motorist. By then it was too late. The surviving victim had been pulled from the burning wreckage. What should have been two clean fatalities and a closed accident file suddenly turned into vehicular manslaughter with dangling threads and probing lawyers who, if they persisted, might find their way back to her. She wanted her software and her equipment back, or better yet destroyed so that no part of it could end up in a crime lab.

She had visions of Lockerbie, where a massive Pan Am passenger jet was brought down by a small explosive device. Two years later scientists in a crime lab managed to identify a single electronic component from the bomb's detonator, a piece of plastic smaller than a baby's fingernail. They traced it back to its point of sale, and from there to two Libyan nationals, who were delivered up by Libyan dictator Muammar Gaddafi.

Ana worried that the same could happen with the equipment she had commissioned if it fell into the hands of the authorities. They would trace it back to its French builders, and from them to her, even though she had never used it. She could end up dressed in an orange jumpsuit in the place the Americans called Gitmo.

The whole thing, the field test, had an air of the unprofessional about it. It had the scent of the American CIA, whose budget was being slashed and whose better operatives were being turned out to pasture in the post–Iraq War world, with other unaligned terrorist groups rampaging through the ruins. She couldn't be sure who the French makers of the equipment were dealing with.

It was true what they said about the Americans. No one could rely on them any longer. They had reached their zenith and were now on the way down, a toothless lion dying in its den. Not only did their government lack the political resolve to defend itself or its allies, it was now missing the basic proficiency to carry out politically sensitive covert operations. To silence those who needed silencing.

A US military clerk with low or no security clearance had taken highly classified government cables, copied them to thumb drives, and delivered them to Internet bloggers for transmission to the public over the World Wide Web. The embarrassment that followed compromised US diplomats removed from their posts, the State Department held up to ridicule, and the National Security Agency exposed for eavesdropping on US allied leaders. Another clerk had stolen top secrets and absconded first to China and then Russia, leaving a trail of confidential American secrets like bread crumbs in his wake. No one knew yet the full extent of the damage, certainly not the American public. Their government was powerless to do anything about it other than downplay it and look for political cover.

At the same time, Washington was awash in amateurish domestic scandals and clumsy cover-ups. To listen to them, every computer the government owned had crashed on cue, coincidentally destroying evidence of government-committed crimes in the process. No one believed the obvious lies—"the spin," as they called it from the White House—but those in power didn't care. They couldn't be prosecuted because they controlled the machinery of enforcement, and to them, that was all that mattered. They had lost all sense of the art, always to provide one's prince with the refuge of credible deniability, what the British called a scintilla of truth.

Ana made a mental note. These people, whoever they

were, were incompetent and, for that reason, dangerous. She would do whatever was possible to learn who they were so that she could avoid doing any business with them in the future. But first she had to recover the laptop, the software, and the small dish antenna that the French mercenaries who built the device had given them to field test.

She finished her coffee, paid the waiter, and grabbed her purse. A minute later she was racing down the street astride the blue Piaggio BV500, helmet on her head, cruising toward the train station and her trip south back to her estate in order to pack for her trip to L.A.

THIS MORNING WE huddle in the conference room at our office, behind Miguel's Concina and the Brigantine Restaurant on Orange Avenue in Coronado.

Pages and files are spread out all over the table as I sit with Harry and our investigator, Herman Diggs, trying to gain a handle on the latest blizzard of paper affecting Alex Ives.

Alex is staying with his mother and father at their home following the bail hearing. This was an exercise that proved to be easier than we thought and is still a mystery to me as to why. There was good news and good news. The first being the apparent lack of knowledge on the part of the cops regarding Ives's connection to Olinda Serna. They seem to be blissfully ignorant of the fact that Ives and his employer were working on a hot news flash in which Serna presumably had a talking role. We don't know the details because Ives still isn't telling us, and his boss has, to date, been unavailable, at least to me. I have left three phone messages for Tory Graves at the *Washington Gravesite*, the digital dirt sheet for which Ives works. None of these have been returned. We assume that if the cops knew about the connection between Ives and Serna, the prosecutor would probably have dumped it on us during the bail hearing, evidence of possible intent in an effort to deny bail. Though this is not a certainty. Using this information in a surprise package at trial could do wonders for a conviction, even if they made no effort to enhance the charges. Letting the jury know that Ives knew Serna and was pursuing her when he passed out behind the wheel and killed her is one of those "wow" factors certain to light up the jury box.

The other happy news was the cost of bail, a mere twenty-five-thousand-dollar bond imposed by the judge, well below the local bail schedule. How this happened is a mystery, though it appeared not to be the doing of the prosecutor as much as the man seated behind him. Beyond the bar rail in the first row of spectator seats was another man, suited up for combat and packing a slick patent-leather briefcase. We found out later this was one of the premium-priced lawyers, a criminal practitioner from Serna's law firm up in L.A.

Apparently they thought enough of her to send somebody down to watch. He conferred with the deputy D.A. over the railing and, after they talked, the prosecutor asked for only twenty-five thousand dollars bail. Even the judge was surprised.

The D.A. then went on to explain that Ives had a job

and family contacts in the community. He even gestured toward Alex's mom and dad sitting behind us, as if the state had produced them, shining character witnesses for the defendant. He told the judge it was a first offense, only marginal evidence of alcohol in the defendant's system. He never even mentioned the French-fried cadaver in the other car, so that by the time he was finished, there was nothing left for me to talk about. I sat there with my thumb in my mouth. If you can't say anything on behalf of your client that is more helpful than what the D.A. has to say, it is best not to say anything at all.

When the judge demanded that Ives surrender his passport and agree not to leave the state pending trial, I looked at the prosecutor wondering if he might object. It was almost as if somebody wanted Ives to skip town and jump bail.

His parents posted the bond out of pocket change. I had a come-to-Jesus moment with the kid outside the courtroom and told him in no uncertain terms not to wander too far. Even if his boss demanded that he travel back east on business, he was not to go. He promised me that he would not, smiled, and they left. Stranger things have happened to me in courtrooms, but not recently. It left me to wonder.

"ACCORDING TO THE accident report, neither driver appears to have applied their brakes prior to impact," says Harry. He has the document prepared by the California Highway Patrol in front of him on the table. "No skid marks on the pavement, though the intersecting road traveled by Ives was dirt until it reached the county highway where they impacted. Still nothing on the pavement to indicate any braking. Serna's rented car was moving at a relatively slow rate of speed, estimated between thirty and forty miles an hour at the point of impact," says Harry.

We are in the process of trying to find out if the navigation satellite system and its proprietors will be able to supply us with any information as to the car Alex was driving and the location of the party that night.

"Let's start with the time of the accident."

"According to the report, the estimate of time is about eleven p.m." says Harry. "The witness who pulled Ives from the burning wreck called it in at eleven-oh-six. He said he tried to get to Serna, but the flames were too hot. That slowed him down on the call."

"What was the speed limit?" I ask him.

Harry flips back one page. "Fifty-five," he tells me.

"So why was Serna going so slow?" I ask.

"Maybe she was looking for something," says Herman. Herman Diggs is a big man, African-American to the soul, former athlete who blew out a knee in college and lost out on a career in football. He has been with us for ten years now, long enough and on such intimate terms that he is now part of the family.

"Not much out there to look for," says Harry. He turns the file toward Herman, who looks at the printout, a satellite photo, probably from Google Maps, showing an overhead shot of desolate desert, a narrow strip of concrete like a gray ribbon running across it with a red marker at the fatal intersection.

"There is the other road," says Herman. He means the dirt strip traveled by Ives. "Maybe she was looking for that."

"You think they were meeting up out there?" I ask him.

Herman shrugs a shoulder. "What did the kid tell you?"

"Nothing. Says he can't remember," I say.

"If they were getting ready to meet, we can be relatively certain that Ives wasn't sitting around waiting for her," says Harry. "According to the report, the estimated speed of Ives's car, a late-model luxury sedan, was approaching eighty miles per hour and accelerating as it entered the highway and impacted the other car. Caved in the entire driver's-side door on Serna's car. Bent it like a pretzel."

"Sounds like a missile," says Herman. "Where'd a kid that age get a ride like that? Must be six figures fully dressed out with all the gadgets and gizmos."

"It was owned by his parents' aviation servicing company," I tell him. "They let him use it from time to time."

"Bet they don't do that again," says Herman.

"According to the accident report, this kind of high speed and acceleration prior to impact is consistent with a driver who has fallen asleep or gone unconscious behind the wheel." Harry is still on point, trekking through the report.

"Still, she makes no effort to evade him. She must have seen him coming," I say.

"On a dirt road doing eighty. That would likely send up a dust trail a blind Indian could follow," says Herman.

"Let me see that photo again," I tell Harry. He passes it over to me. It is difficult to tell from the air, but there doesn't appear to be any elevation, rises that might obscure Serna's vision of the approaching vehicle. No trees or other obstructions.

"She could have been looking at something in her car," says Harry. "A map. Maybe her cell phone. That would explain why she was traveling so slow."

"Maybe." I pass the report back to him.

"More interesting," says Harry, "is the fact that the preliminary toxicology report shows the absence of any drugs in Ives's system."

This was the big surprise of the day. We are all smiles around the table with the news. While it may not cut our client loose entirely, it offers a big headache to the prosecution, who now must explain to the jury how the defendant became unconscious behind the wheel.

The cops are now batting zero for two. No alcohol, at least nothing approaching the presumptive level of intoxication, and no drugs. So that means we have an unconscious client under the influence of nothing.

"Any kind of medical condition," asks Herman, "might account for his problem?"

"Not that we know of," says Harry.

"I asked Ives on the phone this morning and he says no," I tell them. "He's never passed out, never fainted. Had a physical two months ago and passed it with flying colors."

"So what caused it?" says Herman.

"Could have been drugs," I tell him.

"But they didn't find any," says Harry.

"Some of the more complex drugs take a while. Could be weeks before they have a final report. And then there are some they don't even look for in the routine screenings unless there's a reason."

"You mean roofies?" says Herman. "The date rape drug?"

"There's that one and there's others. It is a possibility," I say. "Police don't usually order them up in the normal toxicology screening."

These are known as predator drugs, used by some perpetrators either to engage in sexual assault on the unconscious victim or to rob them. Either way the victim usually remembers nothing when it's over.

They work like conscious sedation and in some countries are used as an anesthetic. Those under their effect lose motor coordination. Their eyes may be open but nothing is being registered in the brain. They result in near total loss of memory during the period that the victim is under the influence.

"Fits the profile of what Ives described as his symptoms," says Harry. "They're absorbed into the system quickly. All trace gone within at most seventy-two hours. They show up in urine tests. Here they drew only blood." Harry's skimming through the report. "Here it is, 'Benzodiazepine.' They didn't check the box, didn't ask for it."

"It's too late now," says Herman.

"I asked Alex about the possibility the last time we

talked to him, you and I at the jail," I tell them. "The question whether somebody might have slipped something to him. It wasn't lost on him. The thought had crossed his mind before I mentioned it. He wondered about the girl, the one who invited him to the party, and whether it was a setup. The single glass of champagne. The fact she never showed at the party. It weighed on his mind."

"I know what you're saying," says Herman. "There's no way Ives coulda driven like hell and gone out into the desert if somebody slipped him a roofie. What that means, somebody delivered him out there. Accident was staged. Is that what you're sayin'? That whoever did it, killed Serna? So there was no mishap involved."

I nod.

"Here we go again," says Harry. "Why can't we just keep this simple? Straightforward DUI with the cops showing no evidence. We push hard enough and they'll kick him loose. Case over. We can move on."

"They nearly did that at the bail hearing," I tell him. "The question is why? Think about it. What do we know?"

"Not much," says Harry.

"On the contrary. We know that Ives was shadowing Serna, not in a physical way, but he had her in the journalistic cross hairs over something. According to Alex, it's big, but for the moment off the record. Somebody drugs him and takes him out into the desert. They smash two cars together, one of them at high speed carrying Alex, the other one with Serna inside. Was she conscious at the time?" I ask.

"What, you think they drugged her too?" says Harry.

"Why not just drown her and dump her on some beach somewhere?"

"Because then there would be evidence. Somebody would have to walk in the sand to dump the body. She might struggle. You'd get bruising, maybe something under her fingernails. This way there is nothing. Major collision and fire. The bodies are burned. If it had worked out the way they planned it, both of them would be dead and we wouldn't be involved to ask any questions."

"You think they were out to get the boy as well?" says Herman.

"Be my guess. Given the reckless nature of the collision. There was certainly no assurance Ives would survive the impact, let alone the fire. The only reason Alex is alive is because a passing motorist pulled him from the wreck. If I had to guess, I would say that our Good Samaritan wasn't part of their opera. Something they failed to plan for."

"You know you're getting paranoid," says Harry. "Soon you'll be seeing black helicopters."

"Give me another theory that explains the events," I tell him.

"OK, tell me one thing," he says. "Both cars were moving. If both Serna and Ives were unconscious, how did they do that?"

I think for a moment, shake my head. "I don't know."

"There you go," says Harry. "Problem with your theory is it doesn't work."

Harry goes back to the accident report, looking for something. He finds the pages and starts to read, running his finger over the paper.

"Have you talked to the kid about this?" says Herman. "The fact that somebody may have tried to kill him?"

"Not in so many words."

"Don't you think you should? Assuming you're right, if they tried once, what's to stop 'em from trying again?"

"Nothing, I suppose."

"He can't run," says Herman. "Can't hide. Bail conditions see to that."

"Yeah. It's all pretty convenient, isn't it?" I tell him.

Herman arches an eyebrow. "So what do we do? Where do we go from here?" He flips open his little notebook ready to jot down whatever little tidbits I can give him.

"Two unknowns," I tell him. "First the mystery girl. We have only a partial name and a description. Asian, very good looking, long dark hair about the middle of her back, about five foot five or five six. First name or nickname, Ben. She has a tattoo on the inside of her left thigh, red and blue, probably a dragon or the tail of a dragon."

Herman is still scribbling on the notepad.

"I would start with the local tattoo parlors."

"Hell, there must be seven thousand of them," says Herman, "and that's only on one block downtown."

"Got your work cut out," I tell him. "Harry and I need to go to work on Alex, to loosen his tongue regarding this hot news tip he's got involving Serna. Makes sense that if that's the only connection between the two of them, and if the accident was staged to trap them both, that the story he was working on is probably the reason."

"OK, tell me this," says Harry. He finally looks up

About the Author

STEVE MARTINI is the author of numerous *New York Times* bestsellers, including *Trader of Secrets, The Rule of Nine, Guardian of Lies, Shadow of Power, Double Tap,* and others featuring defense attorney Paul Madriani. Martini has practiced law in California in both state and federal courts and has served as an administrative law judge and supervising hearing officer. He lives in the Pacific Northwest and is currently at work on the next Paul Madriani novel.

Discover great authors, exclusive offers, and more at hc.com.

from the report. "Says here there is no evidence of mechanical malfunction in the steering or brake systems of either car. And catch this, no evidence of any malfunction or tampering with the accelerator, cruise control, or other speed maintenance systems in either vehicle."

"They can tell all that from the burned-out remains?" says Herman.

"Steel doesn't burn," says Harry. "So, if he was unconscious, on roofies, unable to coordinate his arms or his legs and there was no alteration to the steering, the accelerator, or the cruise control, how did they do eighty miles an hour and steer one car into another in the space of a small intersection? And don't tell me they did it remotely because if they did, there would be evidence of hardware left behind no matter how small it was. The cops would have found it." Harry looks at me across the table, tapping the page of the accident report with his finger.

It is a good question, and one for which I have no answer.